T0165620

Odette

Youssef Cohen

iUniverse, Inc.
Bloomington

Odette

Copyright © 2010 by Youssef Cohen

All rights reserved. No part of this book may be used or reproduced by any means, graphic, electronic, or mechanical, including photocopying, recording, taping or by any information storage retrieval system without the written permission of the publisher except in the case of brief quotations embodied in critical articles and reviews.

This is a work of fiction. All of the characters, names, incidents, organizations, and dialogue in this novel are either the products of the author's imagination or are used fictitiously.

iUniverse books may be ordered through booksellers or by contacting:

iUniverse
1663 Liberty Drive
Bloomington, IN 47403
www.iuniverse.com
1-800-Authors (1-800-288-4677)

Because of the dynamic nature of the Internet, any Web addresses or links contained in this book may have changed since publication and may no longer be valid. The views expressed in this work are solely those of the author and do not necessarily reflect the views of the publisher, and the publisher hereby disclaims any responsibility for them.

ISBN: 978-1-4502-5969-9 (sc)
ISBN: 978-1-4502-5970-5 (dj)
ISBN: 978-1-4502-5971-2 (ebk)

Library of Congress Control Number: 2010913919

Printed in the United States of America

iUniverse rev. date: 12/2/2010

To my son, Max

I

Eleventh Street, Manhattan

In June 1998 I sat at my desk, unable to concentrate on the lecture I was preparing on Machado de Assis's *The Posthumous Memoirs of Brás Cubas*. My copy of the *Memoirs* is well thumbed, as I return often to my favorite passages, to the narrator's quirky puns, jokes, and diatribes, relishing them as one would the habitual gossip of a dear friend. But on that afternoon, Machado de Assis and his narrator had infected me with their melancholy. The office in which I had worked for so many years felt suddenly alien, as if it belonged to someone else, and the hundreds of books I had lovingly arranged side by side now seemed but a meaningless jumble of color and print. The disorientation I felt did not last long, but the lingering sense of futility soon made unbearable the deathly silence of my office. Hoping that a change of place would offer some relief, I picked up the *New York Times* and headed up Broadway toward my favorite coffee shop on Eleventh Street. At the corner of Broadway and Astor Place the sight of green mangos and yellow bananas confused me, for the smell that hung in the pasty heat wasn't of mango but rather of the sausages being fried in the metal stand next to the fruit vendor's. Not far ahead, the Gothic spire of Grace Church rose white in the sky, a giant arrow pointing to the mortals below the way out of their carnal cages.

On Eleventh Street, where my legs had taken me while my mind had drifted, I saw my father standing by the iron bars of the Spanish-Portuguese Cemetery. Impeccably suited in the gray Tasmanian wool he bought in London, a white handkerchief peeking out of his breast pocket, he looked at the worn surface of the stone graves and shook his graying head from side to side slowly, a disconsolate expression stamped on his Mediterranean face. I stood motionless in the speckled shadow of a tree watching him mutter things I could not hear until he walked away and turned the corner onto Sixth Avenue. Only then did I remember it was the sixth anniversary of his death. My father died on my brother's birthday, and on that morning I had made a mental note to call my brother in Brazil, yet my father's death had eluded my memory. Shortly after he passed away, my father began popping up here and there, sometimes on special occasions, often for seemingly no reason at all. In the beginning his apparitions frightened me, but as time went by, my anxiety was gradually replaced by pleasure, the pleasure of watching him without being seen. The years I had spent fearing his stern and critical gaze had worn me out, and many a time I had wished he would disappear, a wish that filled me with guilt when he actually did. Now that I could watch him as if through a one-way mirror, I had the best of both worlds: I could see him without having to endure either his gaze or my guilt. It mattered little whether my father in fact occasionally resurrected or I hallucinated him into being.

At first I attributed the grief that shadowed my father's face to a feeling of kinship with the handful of Sephardic Jews buried under the soft stones of the tiny cemetery. Like them, my father had his roots in the Iberian Peninsula. Both my father's ancestors and the Jews buried on Eleventh Street had fled the Inquisition. The Jews who landed in New Amsterdam in 1654 came from the port of Recife, in northeast Brazil. The Dutch had conquered Recife from the Portuguese in 1630, and under the government of the Dutch West India Company, it became a haven of religious tolerance. Recife Jews began to practice their faith openly. They built a synagogue, schools, and charities, and the records show that Jews were highly organized and deeply involved in the affairs of the community. But when the Portuguese reconquered their port in 1654, the Inquisition now saw Recife Jews, who had converted to Christianity under Portuguese rule, as relapsed heretics. Many were either executed on the spot or sent back to Portugal to be tried by the Holy Office.

Those fortunate enough to escape sailed to Amsterdam, while others sought shelter among the Jewish communities that had been previously tolerated in the more lax colonies of the Caribbean. Among the latter were the twenty-three Jews who landed on the shores of New Amsterdam. After spending weeks at sea, the Jews who made the crossing must have been amazed by what they saw when they reached the Upper Bay. The Hudson Valley and the islands must have looked to them a lush terrestrial paradise. Whales and dolphins escorted the ships entering the bay, and on the land the forests were full of flowers and fruit trees. The woods teemed with wolves, bears, foxes, and other wild animals. September 7, 1654, was 25 Elul, the anniversary of the first day of creation, and upon seeing the verdant landscape on such a day, the newly arrived Jews must have thought of Genesis and a clean beginning. But Stuyvesant did not want them in his little outpost; had it not been for the support of wealthy Jewish merchants from the West India Company, Stuyvesant would have turned them back. The twenty-three Jews stayed, and later more of them came and joined Shearith Israel, a congregation that is now housed in the imposing neoclassical synagogue on Central Park West and Seventieth Street. The Spanish-Portuguese Cemetery of Eleventh Street, at the gate of which my father was shaking his head, was acquired by Shearith Israel in 1804. It was much larger then, but when in 1830 the city opened Eleventh Street, the cemetery was condemned. The congregation petitioned to save the part that wouldn't interfere with the street and was granted its wish. The part of the cemetery that was saved is the miniscule triangle now on Eleventh Street.

My father's ancestors, on the other hand, fled to the Islamic cities of the Ottoman Empire. His paternal grandfather was from Aleppo, Syria, and he, like many Middle Eastern Jews, had moved to Cairo seeking fortune during the cotton boom of the mid-1800s. My father was born in Cairo, in 1915, and so was I, in 1947, and we lived there until the Suez War. In 1956 most of the hundred thousand Jews who lived in Egypt left, and my father took us to Brazil. But he never forgot Egypt. He could not speak of Cairo without sorrow. He missed the city; he loved it, and he gathered the courage to go back one last time only a few years before he died. When I saw him shortly after he returned to Brazil, he acted as if he were no longer of this world.

Perhaps my father shook his head in front of the cemetery because he knew what it meant to leave everything behind, like the New Amsterdam Jews had, or perhaps he regretted that all the other European Jews had not come to the New World before the Nazis got to them. My father himself had narrowly escaped the Nazis in 1942. Fourteen years before he was run out of Egypt, he had run from the Nazis in Paris. Just as they were entering Paris, where he was studying medicine, he was leaving it for Marseille. He remained in this unoccupied city until 1942, when he went to Lisbon and embarked on a ship that took him around the coast of Africa to Cairo. The diary of his voyage around Africa begins in Lisbon on January 20, where he boarded the *Quanza*, a Portuguese ship of seven thousand tons. "We boarded," he writes, "with apprehension. Portugal is neutral yet many of its ships, like ours, are heavily fortified. The *Quanza* sailed at full steam. All the way to Madeira, for two days, the sea was detestable. We were not allowed to visit the island; we admired its dense vegetation and splendid hotels from a distance. Vendors climbed aboard selling canaries for thirty Portuguese crowns a pair. They also sold superb table linens and all manner of mother-of-pearl and tortoise shells."

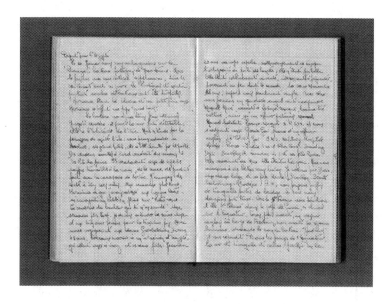

From Madeira the ship sailed to the island of St. Thomas in the Gulf of Guinea, and it is then that my father makes the acquaintance of a few passengers. "With us," he writes, "travels a lady called Diran Garbedian, an Armenian from Egypt who is also going to Suez, and her two daughters. Jeanine, twenty, who has a gorgeous body, is vivacious and provocative, but is unfortunately myopic and forced to wear ugly glasses. Her sister Manouche, fifteen, is also pretty but simple minded. With Alex, my friend from Paris, the four of us became inseparable. There is also Gloria Gai, the wife of an English officer (Lieutenant

Colonel Gai, HMS Military Hospital in Kirkie, Poona, India), and her daughter Roda. Through Gloria I met a Belgian lady and her daughter, Nicole Demblon, a Rhodesian beauty from Salisbury. Alex and I played bridge and danced with them late into the night.

"On February 1 the ship moored at St. Thomas, which saddles the equator. Three days before, as we approached Freetown, an English cruiser flashed signals asking for the name of our ship. 'Good luck,' they answered. Around the equator the sea is as calm as a tranquil lake, but the weather is heavy, very humid, unhealthy. Not a breath of air. Far away the coast of Africa appears wild and deserted. Before our arrival at St. Thomas, as we got to the equator, we had to submit to the usual masked party. A crowned Neptune with a white beard condemned each of us in turn to be thrown into the pool or to a lime bath. It was annoying. Still, I have wonderful memories of St. Thomas. Arriving at night, Nicole and I disembarked, toured the island, and then went to a show in which the ship's orchestra participated. It was one of the most picturesque shows I have ever watched. The dancers wore the local costume. How shall I describe it? It was a mixture of Spanish, Basque, Portuguese, and Brazilian costumes with bright colors that regaled and enchanted the eyes: green mingled with violet and scarlet red. Everything bursts with color in St. Thomas; everything is perfumed; the flowers are large, brightly colored, and fragrant; the green of the trees intense; the fruits huge, juicy, and aromatic. We bought twelve mangos for one escudo, and Alex and I each ate six in a row, which gave us a serious colic. The next morning, we rented two taxis; in the first, Alex, Jeanine, and Manouche; in the second, Mme Garbedian, Nicole, and me. We toured the island, stopping at the most beautiful places. Along the beach coconut trees swayed in the wind, and on the ground fallen coconuts covered the sand. We visited a huge farm, where we found all the fruits of the earth, many of which I had never seen before. The man in charge treated us like kings. He was a mulatto with a white beard who knew Paris and spoke very good

French. Apparently it rains a lot on the island. While we were there it rained three times, intensely; ten minutes later, the sun reappeared, and the island dried. The birds are beautiful. I bought three lovely miniature parrots that entertain us all. At night our ship took to the sea, and large phosphorescent fish followed us for a long time.

"On February 5 we stopped by the shore of St. Antonio de Zaira. A small boat flying a Belgian flag came from the Congo. When the Belgians on board saw their flag, they began to cry. We were moved. No one who hasn't lived the misery of occupation can understand the intensity of this emotion. Under the German boot, Belgians are starving, and their flag is banned from their monuments, palaces, and government buildings. The only flag to be seen is German."

The next day the ship moors at Lobito in Angola, and my father has to say good-bye to Nicole. "We had not made any declarations to each other," he writes, "but we had been inseparable for all this time. She had nicknamed me 'Porcupine.' She came with her parents to say good-bye to us before she disembarked, and when my turn came, she pulled me toward her and kissed me. I was stupefied. I looked at her parents, Alex, Jeanine, and Manouche. I must have looked like an idiot. She had with her the two parakeets I had given her. As the ship slowly left the dock, she waved her arms for more than a quarter of an hour and then ran after us to the end of the dock. It was difficult to leave her. Yet it was also a beautiful moment, a moment of high, intense, and pure feeling. Nicole was twenty-nine years old, yet she was still innocent. She inspired my respect from the moment I saw her. I had asked her once—after dinner on the prow of the ship—if she had ever felt physically attracted to a man. 'Yes,' she said, 'but I cannot imagine kissing a man who will not become my husband.' She was the kind of woman who would make a great companion to a man; the kind you could build a home with. Once, when her parents were dining and she had remained downstairs with a headache, I went to her cabin. She slept on her back with her arms crossed on her breasts, holding a printed copy of my thesis. She slept like Snow White. I left without making a sound."

Nothing much happens between Lobito and Lourenço Marques, Mozambique, except for the terrible seas of the Cape of Good Hope. My father mentions the natural beauty of Capetown, which he sees from afar spread at the foot of majestic mountains. On the eighteenth of February they arrive at Lourenço Marques, a lovely city that became a center of espionage during the war. "The city was close to the South African border," my father writes, "and South Africa was full of German spies. The Boers hated the English and especially the Jews. Our hotel, the Polana Hotel, was full of suspicious-looking people. Mme Garbedian, Jeanine, Manouche, Alex, and I lodged there for more than a month. Our rooms were next to each other, and the heat often forced us to walk around with nothing but towels around our waists, in Abyssinian fashion. Mme Garbedian took me in her confidence and many a time would dry my hair with a towel while I read the newspaper in her room.

"After a few days, in the lobby of the hotel, I met Dr. Schwartz, a psychiatrist from Prague who spoke good French and with whom I became friends. He was a curious man with beady eyes, and since he was a good philosemite, my being a Jew was for him sufficient introduction. Schwartz became infatuated with Jeanine, who by now was Alex's girlfriend. Alex didn't seem inconvenienced. The shrink danced glued to Jeanine's body. 'It's my technique,' he told me. 'Manouche dances well, but Jeanine! Her technique equals mine!' Sardonic as he was, Schwartz made our evenings hilarious, but he could also be nasty. I met a young woman, a physician from Goa, who was a mixture of Chinese and Portuguese, and very beautiful. Schwartz did everything he could to stop me from getting closer to her, but she came to my bedroom anyway when Mme Garbedian and her daughters were out.

"The clipper *Ville de Strasbourg* sailed to Suez on April 10 at six in the morning. Only Alex and I had tickets; the Garbedian family had to wait for another two weeks. The night before we sailed, Alex, Schwartz, and I drank until morning. Schwartz drove us to the dock, with Alex sitting next to him. At one point he told Alex, 'You are very nice, but Jeanine needs a grown man, a guy like me.' Alex patted him on the back amicably. 'Good Dr. Schwartz,' he said, laughing. The scene cannot be described; it was unbelievably funny.

"On April 22, the *Ville de Strasbourg* docked at Aden. We saw nothing of Aden. We stayed there for nearly ten hours, the time necessary to load coal on the ship. The officer who came aboard (Abd El Hamid Ghanem was his name) invited us for a coffee. Happy to talk about himself and his country, he was all smiles, and his hospitality, like that of all Arabs, was irreproachable. At four thirty in the morning, we lifted anchor, and we should be in Port Soudan in three days, to Suez in four, then Cairo, my family, and my house. I am anxious to hug my father, my mother, my little sisters, and my brothers. I haven't seen them in four years; four years that have seen the outbreak of the war and the defeat of France, our France, our second homeland."

At the coffee shop next to the Spanish-Portuguese cemetery, a bare-navel odalisque led the way to a small table between the window and the bar. I sat facing shelves of elaborate pastries, the most attractive of which was a cylindrical mango mousse cake, a good-looking multilayered affair on a crusty chocolate base. I ordered only coffee. The odalisque asked me if I wanted anything else, and after I shook my head, left me alone with the *Times*. I tried to read but could not focus, absorbed as I was by the associations my father's apparition had triggered. His dark face circled in my mind as fiercely as a vulture round its dying prey. He wanted something from me. The odalisque came back with my coffee, and, as I was thanking her, I became aware that I had missed the obvious. When my father shook his head by the gate of the Spanish-Portuguese cemetery he must have been thinking of another cemetery, in Al-Basatin, just outside Cairo. Bassatine Cemetery dates back to the eleventh century, and it is there that my father buried my mother in December 1952—only six years after they wed. Shortly before he died, my father spoke about her for the first, and last, time.

We were sitting among pots of red geraniums on his apartment's terrace in São Paulo when some spirit possessed him, and he began to say things he had never said before. "I married your mother," he said in French, "at the synagogue on Adly Street, in Ismailieh, the European center of Cairo. I tell you, Ismailieh was Paris on the Nile, Paris with palm trees, and Adly Synagogue was the grandest in all of Egypt. I have some pictures." He motioned for me to wait as he stood up and went inside. He returned holding a large photo album bound in burgundy leather. He opened it on his knees and pointed at a picture of a strange building. "This is the Adly Synagogue," he said. "It was designed by an Austrian architect, whose name I don't remember, and was finished in 1903. As you can see, it looked like a pharaonic Art Nouveau temple. The interior of the synagogue was luxurious, with marble

columns, silver lamps in Art Nouveau style, brilliant stained glass, and an elegant stairway leading to the ark. There were Persian rugs everywhere, and for our wedding we put some on the sidewalk, at the entrance to the synagogue. The sanctuary was covered with white flowers. I wore a morning suit with a white carnation in the lapel, and Odette, with a spray of white orchids by her temple, looked like a swan in her white satin dress. It was a magnificent wedding. Many prominent people came, including Egyptian

dignitaries, and Grand Rabbi Nahum Effendi officiated. Even though it wasn't very cold, many women wore furs. They looked like foxes huddled together in the women's corner. I cannot tell you how happy I was, how radiant your mother looked. It was one of the happiest days of my life. Everyone was smiling from ear to ear—my parents, her parents, my brothers and sisters, everyone. The fingers of misfortune had not yet touched us. Odette was a picture of health and beauty; tall, with legs that never ended, dark brown hair, and the blue eyes of a Siamese cat. How could I imagine she'd be gone in a few years?"

My father stopped for a moment and looked away. He stood up, put the album on his seat, and went over to the railing, where he stood quietly for a long while.

When he came back, his thick eyebrows were close together. He rubbed his shoulder and winced from the pain his bursitis was giving him. "Come to think of it," he muttered, "I did have a premonition of sorts. A strange thing happened as my brother Victor and I drove to the synagogue. I looked out the window of the car and saw a huge zeppelin fly over the city. I immediately thought of the Hindenburg disaster. I was twenty-two when it caught on fire. In 1937. We watched the whole thing in the movies, the newsreels. You could see people falling through the flames. The tail burst in fire, and the fire spread through the ship in a matter of seconds. The tail hit the ground first, and then the rest of the ship came crashing down. Men and women with their clothes on fire emerged from the inferno. Some crawled. Some ran. Some stumbled and fell. Anyhow, on the afternoon of my wedding the zeppelin moved so slowly against the hard blue sky that we had the impression it wasn't moving at all—and its immobility unnerved me. It gave me the impression something bad was going to happen. But I forgot all about it as soon as we got to the temple.

"Nineteen fifty-two, the year your mother died, was the worst year of my life, absolutely the worst. It began badly, with the mob burning the city, burning every single building in Cairo that had anything to do with the English, with the foreigner. They poured gasoline over movie houses and torched them—the Rivoli, the Cairo Palace, the Metro. My God! Then they burned down the Shepheard's Hotel, which crumbled into ashes in a few minutes; department stores; bars; nightclubs; the Auberge des Pyramides, the king's favorite casino—you name it. It was a Saturday, Black Saturday. When night fell, a pink cloud lit the sky, and the stench was unbearable. I knew then that it was all over for us. I knew that the English would be kicked out, that Farouk, that degenerate king, was doomed, and with him all of us foreigners and Jews. But we kept hoping things would turn out differently, even after Naguib took over.

"I sent your mother with you and your sister to Europe, just in case. You went to Milan, to stay with my sister Foufy and her husband Leo, and then she took you to Switzerland. I joined you in July, and we all had a good time in Venice. Your mother was so happy in Venice! She had never seen the city before, and San Marco and the Grand Canal seemed a dream to her. We had no inkling of what was coming. Odette complained about stomachaches, but we thought these were minor, normal, and she was fine when we came back to Cairo, at least until October, I think, when she began to have severe chest pains that would not go away. We took her to the hospital in December, where she died on the operating table. The surgeon was my colleague and friend. I know he did his best to remove the abscess under her diaphragm, but she hemorrhaged. They couldn't save her.

"Her death almost killed your grandmother. Marie had a bad stroke, and it took a long time for her to recover. And your grandfather Gad—poor man. She was his only child, his darling. He lit up like a firecracker and threw her a party whenever he caught sight of her. For months he wandered around his apartment in his striped flannel pajamas, pale, gaunt, his beard growing. He was by nature a jovial man, a bon vivant, a champagne drinker who owned several horses and loved pretty women. I had never seen him unshaven before; his cheeks were always smooth, and he smelled of French cologne. You should have seen how this worldly man turned into a hapless infant around his daughter. He simply adored Odette. Because of her he believed in God, miracles, and the goodness of the world. The world, you see, was a beautiful place for him because Odette was in it.

"We buried her in Bassatine, out in the desert. We had the funeral service in a little chapel in the middle of the cemetery. Her body lay in the center of the chapel wrapped in white linen, like a mummy. After the rabbi tore our shirts, we took her to the grave. Gad held out pretty well until she was buried, and then his knees would no longer obey him. Victor and I had to grab his arms and shore him up; he shook like a leaf, poor man—it is awful, you can't imagine, burying your daughter like this. And your grandmother was in the hospital, still recovering from her stroke.

"We built a high iron fence around Odette and my parents' graves. I decided I would turn the little plot into a beautiful garden, and so I did. I planted orange trees and roses that climbed on a trellis behind your mother's grave and hired some people who lived nearby to water the plants and flowers during the week. Gad and I went out there most weekends. I can see him as if it were yesterday, with the hose in his hands, happy among the rose bushes. In a couple of years the garden grew into a veritable oasis in that arid cemetery that was nothing but stone and dust. You could see the trees from far away, a patch of green in the sandy plain, and it was a real pleasure to drive up to the little garden and enter through its pretty gate into the perfumed shade of the trees.

"Bassatine is nothing but rubble now. When I went back in 1985 all the marble that used to cover the graves had disappeared. Row after row of graves, for miles, were half-broken, ruined. Thank God, the few Jews who stayed behind were able to save Bassatine. There are probably no more than a hundred Jews left in Cairo, mostly older women, and one of them, Carmen Weinstein, told me that the marble had been stolen in the sixties and is now part of the luxurious hotels that were built then on the banks of the Nile. Bassatine had also been invaded by squatters, and one of them, an auto mechanic, had built his shop close to Odette's grave. This is not unusual in Cairo, you know. The poor build their homes among the graves, making veritable cities out of Cairo's immense cemeteries. Carmen managed to get some help from Israel, the Egyptian government, and wealthy Egyptian Jews and kicked the squatters out of the cemetery. A man called Jacques Hassoun—who lives in Paris and who, by the way, published a beautiful book called *Les Juifs D'Egypt*—organized Egyptian Jews to preserve the cemetery. He helped Carmen a lot. When I was in Cairo she told me they were going to build a wall around the place and begin to identify the graves. My brother Jacques and sister Foufy had already located Odette's and my parents' graves and had put new marble plaques on them with names and dates, all in Arabic."

My father told me this not long before he died, and I had listened in a state of semishock. He had never spoken about my mother's life or death, nor had my grandparents, nor had anyone else, for that matter, and for some reason, which as I heard my father speak struck me as unfathomable, I had never asked. As he reminisced I became aware that I had participated in a conspiracy to keep my mother's name unspoken. Even after my father had blurted out his feelings, I dared not ask any questions. Some unreasonable fear gripped me whenever I thought to inquire about my mother, as if to do so were dangerous to my own and my family's survival. It was as though to make my father or grandparents speak of her would cut the tenuous threads that tied us together, and I would find myself suddenly adrift, homeless.

As I sipped my coffee and reflected on my silent complicity, I remembered a Bosch drawing that had lodged itself deep in my memory. On the bare branches of a dead tree, birds screech and flap their wings. Perched in its hollow trunk is an owl, and below it, within an opening at the base of the tree, lies a fox. In the background, among the forest trees, stands a huge pair of human ears, and in the foreground seven open eyes gaze at us from the earth. The drawing is a visual metaphor of Bosch's hometown—Hertogenbosch, from which he took his brush name. *Hertog* is the word for duke, and *Bosch* is that for forest, and so Bosch's hometown can be translated as *duke's forest,* and the drawing is telling us that it is a dangerous place, for the duke's forest has ears and eyes. In a place of this sort it is better to be silent and hide, like the wise owl and the cunning fox, than to screech and flap one's wings like the exotic birds on the branches of the dead tree.

The seven eyes looking up from the ground haunt me, as do my father's eyes. I wish I could have cut a path through the thistles of my fear straight to my father's heart and asked him more questions about my mother. Maybe this would have given me richer memories, for these are the blood of old age. As the odalisque put a second cup of coffee in front of me, I wondered if she could see the regret in my eyes. Packed together, all my memories of my mother weren't dense enough to bring her back to life. The thought that I would never remember my mother, that I had lost her forever, made me feel like the toddler I had read about, I can't recall where, who, having lost his mother, had tied a long string around the receiver of a telephone, run it through the hallway, passed it around the legs of his bed, and tied it to the antenna of a portable radio which he had placed on the sill of his open window. When asked why he had done this, the boy told his father he was waiting for his mother to call him from the sky.

The image of this frantic child wiring his room disquieted me. I was about to ask the odalisque for my check when the young woman sitting at the table next to mine caught my attention. She wore chic narrow glasses, through which she was peering at a burst of color on the page of a book, a burst that I recognized as a reproduction of David Hockney's *Pearblossom Highway.* This photocollage was part of Hockney's project to improve upon conventional photography, which he thought failed to represent the world as we see it. Hockney first experimented with Polaroid shots, snapping details of his house and friends, and arranging the overlapping photos into compositions that can be seen as an integrated whole. These Polaroid composites solved some of his problems with photographs, in that they offered multiple points of view, all in focus, and allowed the viewer to build separate glimpses across time into one continuous coherent whole. But the Polaroids, with their rectangular edges, still failed to put the viewer inside the world. They could not represent the world as our vision does—without edges. Influenced by Picasso and the Cubists' attempt to break down edges, Hockney moved beyond the grids of his composite Polaroids and invented the photocollage, a fluid composition that puts the viewer inside the world it depicts and that often contains a narrative, not unlike the medieval paintings that depict the episodes of Christ's life all on one single panel. Hockney made many wondrous photocollages, but the one that moves me the most portrays his mother in the cemetery outside Bolton's Abbey.

On that peculiar afternoon at the coffee shop, I beheld Hockney's mother's collage in my mind, almost photograph by photograph, as if it were right in front of my nose. The woman in the fancy glasses had closed the book and left, and I was lost in the dewy pelt of grass beneath Mrs. Hockney's shoes just a few feet away from her son's own wingtips. Hockney had put himself, or rather his shoes, in the picture, taking us to Bolton Abbey to meet his mother. And as I looked at her, so meticulously portrayed, loving picture overlapping loving picture, old stone graves and Abbey ruins in the background, her sadness—she and her husband would come to the abbey when they were courting—made me want to put my arm around her shoulder. At the same time I envied Hockney his good fortune. He was lucky to have had the chance to make such an intimate portrait of his mother, to have been so close to her and for as long as he had.

The desire to portray my mother in the same way gripped me with such force that I decided I would compose a photocollage of her. To make one I needed a series of pictures of the same event taken from different vantage points, and it seemed to me that I had such a

series in the small collection of Odette's wedding pictures Uncle Victor had given me shortly after my father died. I'd have to cheat, I thought; I'd have to crop the pictures and resize the photos. But I didn't mind, as cheating seemed an insignificant price to pay to bring Odette back to life.

I settled the bill and rushed back home. Armed with my Mac, a Canon scanner, scissors, and glue, I went to work—and as I worked with her pictures, and looked closely at the details of her face, I grew even more aware of how little I remembered of my mother. We must have been close once, but now only a vaporous memory remained of those early affections. My photocollage could not unveil the mystery that is my mother, but it did, nevertheless, offer some consolation. I could feel what she went through, from her initial nervousness to the final burst of a joyful smile.

For obvious reasons, I couldn't put my shoes or any other evidence of my presence in the collage's little narrative—even though I was probably there. My parents were married on December 9, 1946, and I was born on July 27, 1947, and no one has ever told me I was early.

II

San Nicolò di Lido, Venice

I arrived at Marco Polo Airport in the early afternoon of a hot September day. The arrows pointing toward the Alilaguna boat to Venice drew me into a labyrinth of deserted alleys and shuttered warehouses, a long ghostly succession of sun-drenched walls and sharp turns. At the end of an unnamed street a line of people inching its way into the bowels of a boat finally came into view. Inside the cabin I leaned my head against a window and, lulled by the gentle rocking of the boat, fell into a light sleep. The Doge's Palace floated high above the green waters of the lagoon, and the Marangona, the bell that from the top of the Campanile had for centuries announced the beginning and end of the workday, rang nostalgic in my ears. The boat made its way among the islands, and from time to time, as it docked alongside the undulating stations, I would open my eyes, and the images and sounds of my dream mingled with visions offered by the shimmering lagoon.

Only after the boat left the Lido station of Santa Maria Elisabetta and aimed its prow at San Marco was I able to keep my eyes open. As we approached the Piazzetta I looked up at the Ducal Palace and noted with the usual affection the traceried windows close to the Bridge of Sighs. I cannot remember when I

first noticed these lower windows in the sea façade. It seems that I have been aware of the two lone windows for a very long time, and I wouldn't be surprised to learn that I noticed them when I came to Venice with my mother in the summer of 1952, a few months before she died. Beyond eyewitness reports, there is no trace of her after she left Venice. Odette's last snapshots were taken from the Piazzetta; her last letter is the one she wrote just before she went to Venice, and the last stamps on her passport mark her exit from Venice and her reentry to Egypt. The only vivid memory I have of my mother is of her bronzed calves and white sling-back sandals as she is climbing out of a motor launch onto the Piazzetta. This may be a fabricated memory, an illusion based on a story or a picture; yet, if I close my eyes, I can feel the boat bobbing in the water, smell the salty air, and almost touch the white strap hugging her ankle.

The Alilaguna boat slowed and sent a wave of filth slapping against the platform of San Zacharia's stop. Dragging my suitcase over the bridge, I stopped on the Piazzetta more or less where the last snapshot of my mother was taken. In the photo she stands in a puddle of pigeons between corn vendors and an old camera on its tripod. Only months away from the mortal illness so eerily presaged by the nurselike vendors and the camera's black cloth, Odette poses

for the classic tourist shot. Like her, throngs of people around me were now being photographed with pigeons. They enacted this strange ritual with great pleasure, completely oblivious to the effects of pigeon overcrowding. Corralled in large numbers, as they are in Venice, the birds become susceptible to parasites that can cause pneumonia, toxoplasmosis, and salmonella. But none of the people inducing the birds to flutter over their hands or perch on their arms seemed to mind. The tourists were having fun, and fun often requires a suspension of one's critical faculties, or so I thought as I cut a swath through the crowd and hurried toward the arcade of the Procuratie Vecchie. I passed the Caffè Quadri's musicians, who, sweating in their usual black-tie attire, were playing *Blue Danube,* and headed toward the passageway that took me to my hotel in the quiet Corte Sorzi. Standing by the Corte's well, three French women were talking about an exhibit at the Guggenheim. One of them, a lean blonde with trendy short hair, held a leash, at the end of which was a tiny terrier. As I walked around them, the dog crouched and relieved himself. The blonde turned around and grinned. "Bravo, Matisse!" she cheered.

The next morning I dragged my jet-lagged limbs to a café. I ate a cheese sandwich under a large umbrella and then boarded a vaporetto to San Nicolò on the Lido. Later in the afternoon I was to meet Aunt Foufy, my father's youngest sister, and her husband Leo, who were staying at the Hotel des Bains. Aunt Foufy had put my mother up in her small apartment in Milan from mid-April to the end of June 1952. My mother's letters, the only records of her voice and handwriting, have as their return address Aunt Foufy and Uncle Leo's Milan apartment on Via Adelaide Ristori 1. I had no intention of interrogating Aunt Foufy. On the contrary, I hoped that by letting her speak freely, some vivid memory of my mother would make itself known to my mind. But I hadn't seen my aunt for many years, and the thought that our encounter might be punctuated by awkward silences and disturbing revelations filled me with apprehension. I decided to busy myself during the couple hours before we met by revisiting the Antico Cemitero Israelitico, the old Jewish cemetery adjoining the Monastery of San Nicolò.

As the vaporetto left San Marco, I stood on the crowded deck at the stern watching the contours of the palace blur and dissolve. Farther into the lagoon, I sought shelter in the shade of the passenger cabin, and when the vaporetto docked at San Nicolò, I reluctantly went out into the glare of the sun.

The cemetery wall was across the street from the vaporetto stop. A man stood by the gate waiting, as I was told he would be. He readily introduced himself as Guido, the person who would take me on a tour of the grounds. We waited a few minutes, and as it became evident that I would be his only customer, he unlocked the gate and let me inside. Although the tree-shaded graveyard offered a welcome relief from the burning sun, I was disappointed by the orderliness that surrounded me. That the cemetery had undergone restoration since I had first seen it was not news to me, yet I could not have imagined it as tidy as it now appeared. When I first saw it the graveyard had the wild look of a recently discovered archeological site. The graves were scattered about, half-swallowed by growing shrubbery, and wind and rain had carved their own marks alongside the Hebrew letters on the lichen-stained stelae. Now the restored tombstones stand straight on a tree-shaded green lawn. A touch too composed, the cemetery has acquired the artificial look of a museum, as if the dead and their abodes had been slicked up for the camera.

At once mourning the old burial ground's mysteries and celebrating its rejuvenation, I followed the guide, a short, dark, hirsute man with a friendly smile, as he explained that the cemetery had once stretched across the Lido from the lagoon to the Adriatic. Since the early fifteen hundreds, when Jews were forced to live in the ghetto at the opposite end of Venice, the dead were ferried by gondola around the whole length of the northern edge of the city and across the district of Castello out to the

Lido. To keep down the costs of this lengthy passage by boat, as well as to avoid attracting unwanted attention, funerary corteges were usually limited to two gondolas or barges. Despite these efforts, the corteges still met with harassment. When the corteges passed under the Bridge of San Pietro di Castello, then the seat of the patriarch, hostile crowds threw trash at the Jews rowing their brethren to their final rest. To avoid the mob, the Jewish community obtained permission to dig a canal that circumvented the bridge, a canal that was called Canal degli Ebrei.

Guido told me all of this in Italian, slowly pronouncing each syllable, before he began to interpret the images sculpted on the tombstones. He pointed at the hands open in benediction, fingers joined two by two and thumbs extended out, and noted that they represented the Kohane, descendents of the high priests of old. The pitcher from which water fell into the bucket for ritual cleansing represented the Levites, descendents of the tribe to which this task was assigned. And the deer in the basket may have been an allusion to Moses, whose mother had placed him in a basket to save him from the soldiers of Pharaoh and the waters of the Nile. Guido skipped other markings (there were too many symbols to account for in one visit) and stopped in front of a small, unadorned tombstone.

"This is the grave of a great man," Guido said, his whole being ablaze like a maple tree in autumn. "Rabbi Leon da Modena is buried here; he died in 1648. He was an extraordinary teacher and writer, but unfortunately he had a bad addiction. *Le carte,* you know; he liked gambling a little too much, and he had very bad luck. Look at the tombstone. It is a piece of a window, as you can see from the moldings here in the back. The rabbi died in poverty. He didn't have enough money to buy a proper stone. But he wrote this beautiful book called *Historia de' Riti Hebraici*, in which he explains Jewish rites and customs to the gentiles. The book was printed in both Paris and Venice, and it received praise from William Boswell and King James I. Rabbi Modena did a great service to Jews, because in those days people were ignorant about us and thought we had rituals to drain the blood of gentile children and put it in our matzos. The rabbi also helped the Amsterdam Jews fight the heresies that plagued their community. In the seventeenth century there were many Marranos in Amsterdam, you know, like the famous philosopher Spinoza, who opposed the authority of the rabbinate, the Mishnah, and the Talmud. These heretics claimed that the oral law distorted the Torah. The rabbis, who wanted to excommunicate these people, appealed to Leon da Modena, and he wrote major works that refuted the heretics. If you have time, you should visit the Ghetto Nuovo. They have tours that start at the museum, and there is a good library there."

With these words, our tour was over. We stepped outside, and Guido locked the gate. He gave me his business card, thanked me for the tip, and left for the vaporetto stop. I watched him with a surge of affection as he stopped at the curb and looked in both directions, carefully, as if a rogue car could suddenly appear in the deserted street and run him over.

I arrived a quarter of an hour early at the Hotel des Bains. The sun, though mercifully lower, still shone hot in the haze above the hotel. I thought this appropriate. The Hotel des Bains is, of course, the stage for Thomas Mann's novella, *Death in Venice*, and heat and haze figure so prominently in Professor Aschenbach's story that I have come to associate the hotel with oppressive weather. A crisp blue sky above its art deco façade would be strangely dissonant and disorienting. I entered the hotel's front garden and climbed the stairs to the seaside terrace. My intention was to have a drink at the bar, but as I stepped into the high-ceilinged lobby I could not tear myself away. Professor Aschenbach had materialized among the large potted palms and plush furnishings that had once filled the luxurious room. He sat in a black leather armchair peering behind his newspaper at Tadzio, the beautiful boy he had just noticed. In his English sailor's suit, Tadzio sat with his sisters around a wicker table, his elbow propped on the arm of his chair and his face resting on his fist.

Thomas Mann had met the real Tadzio, Wladislaw Moes, in this same room. In May of 1911, Thomas, his wife Katia, and his brother Heinrich lodged for a week at the then sumptuous Hotel des Bains. Heinrich, by the way, was well known for his novel *Professor Unrat* (*The Blue Angel*) which tells the story of a schoolmaster whose love for a cabaret singer—much like Professor Aschenbach's love for Tadzio—ruins him. On the first evening of the Manns' stay, among the elegant crowd waiting for dinner in the lobby, Thomas noticed eleven-year-old Wladislaw. He was apparently as smitten with the boy as Aschenbach would be with Tadzio, an infatuation that did not escape his wife's notice. Katia noted that her husband had a weakness for the boy, whom he liked to watch play on the beach, though she did not think Thomas followed the youth through the streets and bridges of Venice— as Aschenbach would Tadzio. Thomas surrendered neither to the boy's charms nor to the voluptuousness of doom. Unlike Aschenbach, when news of a cholera outbreak in Palermo reached them, Thomas, his wife, and his brother left the Lido in a hurry.

As Thomas, Katia, Heinrich, Aschenbach, Tadzio, his governess, and his sisters sat among the well-appointed crowd that now filled the palatial lobby of my disordered imagination, a flutter of panic went through me. The Hotel des Bains, or for that matter all of Venice, seemed but a grand mausoleum. It was as if I had come to Venice to meet the dead, and they were now beckoning me to join them wherever they lived. I recalled my father telling me how he had awoken in a cold sweat terrified by a dream in which his parents had appeared to him. What?! they had raged. You are not going to abandon us again, are you? Surely the city's power to conjure up my mother's death, the earlier visit to the Jewish cemetery, as well as the ghosts haunting the hotel, bore much of the responsibility for my momentary dread. But most of all, as I can now see in hindsight, I had an unreasonable fear of what my aunt might reveal, as though some ugly secret lay at the bottom of my mother's premature death. On the threshold of the seaside terrace, I feared for my life, as if what I was about to learn from my aunt would be as fatal as the Asiatic cholera that killed Aschenbach on a beach chair by the cabanas across the street. Although I had not seen them for twenty years or so, I recognized my aunt and uncle instantly. Despite her advanced age, Aunt Foufy had retained her coquettish looks and Uncle Leo the astonishing full head of hair and debonairness that had given him a reputation as a ladies' man. Time had left its mark, no doubt; their skin had lost its luster and had wrinkled, their hair thinned and grayed. Yet, so much had resisted time that I had the impression they had been artificially aged by a makeup artist. They sat in the shade of the awning at a table near the verandah's balustrade, she in a lavender blouse, a string of pearls around her neck, and he in a navy blue polo shirt, in the same spot I imagined Aschenbach sat in his white suit as he watched the rascally balladeer sing a buffo baritone on the front lawn. They did not see me as I approached the table, not until my shadow made them turn toward me. Uncle Leo stood up and hugged me, followed by Aunt Foufy, who kissed me on both cheeks.

"He is the spitting image of Albert," Uncle Leo said, in the nasal French of the Levantine Jews. "For a moment there," he continued, "I thought I was in front of a ghost. I see you also keep yourself in good shape—just like your father. He was obsessed with his body." Obviously embarrassed, Aunt Foufy nudged her husband. Leo turned toward her, affecting surprise. "Why?" he said. "It's true. When he was young, Albert did Greco-Roman wrestling and lifted weights. A true Tarzan, he was. He wanted to be like Johnny Weissmuller. Do you remember Weissmuller? Maybe you were too young. To tell you the truth, I myself was fond of Cheetah. Anyway, it's really nice to see you. I hope that we'll get to see more of each other from now on." Uncle Leo paused and stared at me. "Amazing," he said. "You are a fair-skinned facsimile of your father."

We sat down and ordered a bottle of pinot grigio. Aunt Foufy directed Leo to change places with me. "Come sit close to me," she said, and as I did, she rubbed my arm and patted my hand. "It's so good to see you," she whispered. We made small talk until the wine came, and then we drank to our reunion. "I remember you as a boy," Aunt Foufy said, "when you came to Milan with your mother. Leo and I, and our first daughter, Nadia, lived in a small two-bedroom apartment, and Odette and your Aunt Jeanne, who also had two small children, came at the same time, so we were literally on top of each other. It was very cramped, but only for a couple days, because your mother and Jeanne took you and your sister and your cousins to a home close to Gryon in Switzerland. The home was called Bambi, I think—it was a sort of small camp for children. They called them 'homes' in those days." Aunt Foufy reached into her leather tote bag and pulled out a pair of reading glasses and a manila envelope. "Here," she said, putting on her glasses and opening the envelope, "I brought you a picture of Odette clowning around in Venice with your father.

"It was a pleasure to hear Odette laugh. I remember how she laughed when we went to see *Don Camillo* with Fernandel. Fernandel played a Catholic priest battling the Communist mayor of a small town, and the priest, Don Camillo, had these amusing conversations with Jesus. He would look up at the crucifix above the altar and complain aloud that the Communists had given him a beating, and the booming voice of Jesus told him to stop whimpering. 'What's a little beating?' Jesus would say. Odette laughed so hard it was embarrassing, but her laughter set other people laughing. The way she laughed was even funnier than the movie. What a shame. Odette was so young. She was a handsome woman, with dark, Spanish good looks and striking blue eyes. We called her Josephine Baker because she was so tall and tanned. She was smart and lively and knew how to have a good time; people liked to be around her. She didn't like Milan that much; the weather was awful, it rained a lot; but she loved the lakes. We took her to Lugano, Cuomo, and Stresa. I recall her being very excited with Stresa. She thought Isola Bella was romantic and beautiful, and she wished Albert were with her. We weren't as lucky with the other places around the lake as we were that Sunday in Stresa. It was a gorgeous day, breezy and crisp, with a glorious sun shining over the lake, and everyone was joking, in a terrific mood. That Sunday, Odette was radiant, and even I, who was going through a rough patch, felt cheerful. I almost forgot about my problems.

"Even in Milan, in spite of the rain, we had some good times together. We'd do the groceries together, or go shopping and visit the sites. Odette wanted to go everywhere; she didn't like staying home much. I was having a very difficult time, and she did her best to keep me company and cheer me up. This is not to say that we didn't have our little fights. The only one who didn't have any problems with Odette was Leo here. He loved her and took her around in his beloved Lambretta because, you know, Odette was a bit of a flirt, and she always said wonderful things about him. I liked her too, but there were things about her that got on my nerves."

Aunt Foufy chuckled and then hesitated, caught as she was between a fear to give offense and a reluctance to sugarcoat the truth.

"Odette helped with everything, the cleaning, cooking, shopping, etcetera, but she was very fussy, and she had a compulsive need to keep drawers and surfaces tidy. Her complaints about disorder were tiresome. She was also constantly worried about her appearance, sometimes to the point of being childish. I remember the day she sent a beautiful white dress with a pattern of flying black swallows to the cleaners, and they ruined it. They washed it instead of dry cleaning it, and it shrunk. Odette complained about this for days on end. It was a pretty dress, for sure, but there was no reason for all this drama; it wasn't the end of the world. Odette was an only child, and I think that in some ways she may have been a little spoiled. Very fastidious, she took hours to dress. Well, maybe I'm being unfair. I don't want to give you the wrong impression; I'm just telling you how I remember it. I liked Odette. I still feel guilty sometimes about not having treated her better, but I wasn't in the best of moods. My mother had just died. There were other things too. Leo and I were involved with politics at the time, and Odette wasn't political at all, which made me impatient with her. We were Socialists, you know, and that's in part why we left Egypt earlier."

Foufy glanced at Leo knowingly. Her glance conveyed layers of meaning accumulated over half a century of marriage that only they could fully disentangle. "I don't know if you are aware of this," Aunt Foufy said, "but in Egypt there were many Communist Jews who didn't identify either with the Zionists or the Nationalists. We did side with the anticolonial struggle of Egypt against the British and Farouk, but our ultimate aim was to free people from the horrible poverty and servitude in which they lived, and still do, as I'm sure you know. The formation of the state of Israel and the new Arab nationalism complicated things for Jewish Communists like us. Nobody wanted us anymore. We were criticized by the non-Jewish Communists and by the Zionists as well, and persecuted by the government. But I'm sure you know all of this. As I was saying, I was in a terrible mood because my mother, your grandmother Sara, had died a few months before. Mother and I were very close because I was the youngest. My brothers and sisters were all much older than I, and naturally they weren't around the house as much as I was. Until my late teens, when we moved to the center of the city, we lived in Sakakini, across the street from Sakakini Palace. You must go there when you go to Cairo. The building we lived in is no longer there, but the palace is still standing, in very bad shape, but still standing.

"Here are some pictures I brought you," Aunt Foufy said as she pulled out some smaller photos from the manila envelope. "This is mother on the terrace of our apartment. Mother had reddish hair, even redder than yours, and green eyes. She stood out in the crowd in Egypt, just like you did when you were a child. The apartment was immense, and the terrace was twenty feet long. My father loved it. Early in the mornings he would sit on the terrace and drink his coffee, and at night he would go out on the terrace to smoke his last cigarette of the day. Saturdays, when he could avoid work, he fell asleep there with the newspaper on his lap." Aunt Foufy brought one of the photos closer to her face and pointed at the rococo structure in the background. "I can't see very well because of my glaucoma," she said, "but I think that's Sakakini Palace, behind my mother. Do you see it? It is a baroque building, built like an extravagant wedding cake, the home of Habib Sakakini. He was a

Greek Catholic from Syria who made a lot of money selling cats. Yes, cats. At the time, Suez was infested with rats, and Habib sold the government thousands of cats. My father knew him well. Papa worked as the manager of the Mohamed Ali Club, a fancy club where the important people gambled.

"Habib was made a count by the king, and after that he was addressed as Count Sakakini Pasha. The count kept peacocks in the garden, and at dusk they would come out of their kiosks and spread their tails. It was a magnificent spectacle. You know, Cairo is the color of sand, and to see these gilded, turquoise tails glowing under a pink sky was a feast to the eyes. We would go out on the terrace just to see them.

"When I was little I spent a lot of time with my mother and the cook, who was also Jewish, helping with small tasks like making *mahshi*. I cored the green peppers and stuffed them with rice, ground meat, currants, and pine nuts. The smell of chopped onion and pine nuts frying in olive oil was wonderful. My mother kept a strictly kosher house. The Jewish butcher, Malki I think, who had a shop up the street, delivered the meat every morning to the house. We observed Shabbat. From Friday evening to Saturday night mother never cooked or used electricity. But she was raised like a true Arab, and unlike my father and us, who spoke several languages, she spoke only Arabic. Although she was a religious and observant Jew, she had a curious habit. I often went with her to one mosque or another to pray at the tomb of a great sheik. When we summered at Tanta, a town in the Delta, she always prayed at the el-Badawi tomb. Sidi Ahmed el-Badawi is one of the most venerated Sufi saints in Egypt. Many centuries ago he had a vision that told him to go to Tanta, and there he lived like an ascetic on the roof of a house. Mother told me that his disciples were called *ashab el-sath*, which means 'people of the terrace.' The saint died on the terrace and was buried there, and later a mosque was built to incorporate the mausoleum. Every year the saint's birthday is celebrated in Tanta with a great *moulid*. Moulids are beautiful, full of color and bright lights. After they visit the saint's mausoleum, the revelers chant Allah's name until they go into a trance. At night they light up lanterns, and there are puppet shows and processions for a whole week. It's something. Tanta's I think is Egypt's largest moulid. I was told that nowadays two million revelers attend the festival at the end of the cotton harvest. My mother was very taken by the saint; I'm not sure why or how. I think it had something to do with the fact that she was an orphan and was raised by an uncle, but I don't know the details."

43

Moved by some distant vision of her red-haired mother in a dusty street of old Tanta, Aunt Foufy swallowed hard. "Mother also practiced charity," she continued, "and was devoted to her poor. Once or twice a week we went in a horse-driven carriage to Haret el Yahoud, the old Jewish quarter in the heart of Islamic Cairo, to take old clothes, food,

and money to poor families she knew. I enjoyed these trips because I often sat in front, and the driver sometimes let me hold the reins. Mother did everything she could to get extra money for her poor. She enlisted my sister Jeanne's or one of my brothers' help to increase the prices of things on the accounts she presented to my father. He sometimes noticed what she had done and criticized her, which usually led to an argument. Mother said she enjoyed these morning arguments; for some reason they amused her. We sometimes gathered in the adjoining room and laughed as we listened to my mother's provocations and my father's complaints. They argued back and forth for fifteen minutes or so, and he would always capitulate. She always managed to get her extra piastres for her poor. Mother was fun and full of energy until diabetes killed her zest for life. When I left Egypt she no longer went to the Opéra or the Théâtre Nacional, which she loved so much; nor even to the Cinéma Métropole or the Weber, the elegant movie theatres she used to frequent in the past. I was away in Milan when she died. Albert, your father, sent me a moving letter. I made a photocopy for you. Your poor father had no idea that he would bury his wife only a year after he buried his mother. Why don't you read it while I go to the ladies' room?"

I stood up and moved my chair back to let her pass. Aunt Foufy handed me the letter, and, holding Uncle Leo's arm, walked away cautiously, afraid, I imagine, that her failing eyesight might trip her at any moment.

Written in green ink on the pale yellow stationery of my father's clinic, the letter begins in the direct, unsparing manner in which my father broke unpleasant news: "Mother passed away this Monday at 23:30. She suffered a great deal. Her heart could no longer pump the blood that stagnated in her lungs, and her lungs were oppressed by the liquid accumulating in the pleurae. She struggled to breathe. I have rarely seen so much energy and strength, such a will to live. For a whole week, Celine and Tolla sat by her bed. Her nights were horrible, intolerable. The evening prior to her death I took her to the hospital. She was at the end of her rope. At nine o'clock Jeanne, my sister, Jeanne Weinstein, Esther Agami, and Odette left her after a short visit. Then she began to scream. I tried to reason with her, to plead with her not to scream, for the sake of the other patients. 'I cannot stop,' she said. 'I'm going to try.' She was indomitable. My God, what strength, what energy. She would hug me tightly so as not to scream, and for an instant, through her glassy eyes, imploring and looking without seeing, her once expressive, lively, kind gaze, and even her smile, shone through. I gave her another shot of morphine, to relieve her. She relaxed and was able to talk. 'My children and husband are all alone,' she said and slept. In the dark and silence of the night I listened to her breathing. It was slow and regular. To the end I kept hoping she would escape. From time to time I could no longer hear her respiration, and I would look at her anxiously. But she'd start again. Then a cry in the night, 'Mother, mother, my heart.' She thrashed about in bed, and then it was over. She was in my arms and I was paralyzed. Her features relaxed and rest penetrated her body. She was so small, like a child. What a hideous moment. I felt as though the earth had collapsed over me."

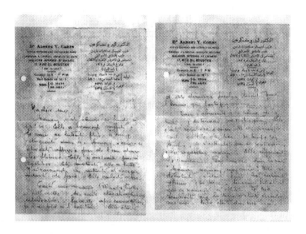

I was glad to have time to recompose myself before my aunt and uncle reappeared and made their way across the weary elegance of the lobby. I helped Aunt Foufy to her seat, and after she was comfortably installed in her chair, I told her the letter had shaken me. I had seldom heard my father express his feelings so openly. Aunt Foufy nodded and brushed my cheek with her fingers. "I can't imagine," she said, "what it must have been like for you to lose your mother so suddenly, so young. You know, in Milan Odette often complained about a pain in her stomach, and she went to see several physicians. I thought she was behaving a bit like a spoiled child; that being alone in Milan, without her husband and kids, she wanted some attention. So I told her it was probably nothing. One of the doctors she saw thought something was wrong with her gallbladder. He gave her injections and pills, but the discomfort wouldn't go away. Your father and your Uncle Victor, who was also a physician, thought it wasn't serious. Odette told me that Albert wanted to have another child, another girl, but she insisted on being cured of her ailments before getting pregnant. My God, when I think about it I feel guilty; it's been more than forty years, and I still get these pangs of guilt. She looked perfectly healthy, so we didn't believe her; we treated her like a fussy child. Obviously something must have been terribly wrong, and as it turned out, it was some kind of abdominal abscess that killed her. We were dumbfounded when we heard. Leo and I were so shattered by the news that we didn't know what to say. Everything that people usually say on these occasions seems so silly. Nothing could express the pain and shock we felt. We refused to accept the reality of what had happened; we just couldn't, and it was a little out of cowardice, also, that we didn't write a letter to your father until months had passed. We didn't know what to say to him, how to console him. Your mother's disappearance at the age of thirty was too cruel, beyond consolation. She was lovely, full of life. How could this happen? I think Albert never recovered, not really. He went about his life never complaining, but everyone noticed he wasn't the same man. Something inside him hardened. It's difficult to explain these things. You just feel them. What can I tell you? Your mother adored you and lavished affection on you and your sister." Aunt Foufy smiled sadly. "You were such a shy and quiet child, my dear, and from the looks of it you haven't changed. You stayed in the background quietly watching everybody."

Night had fallen when I reached the vaporetto station of Santa Maria Elizabetta. Not a shred of cloud roamed the sky. A vast inky dome stretched far over the black waters of the lagoon to the twinkling lights that fringed San Marco. The black expanse of water and sky discouraged me. It reminded me of the darkness in which my past seemed forever buried. The traces of the short

47

years I shared with my mother—the photos, letters, witnesses— were real enough, and so were the intimations, dreams, and unmistakable feelings. Yet I was at pains to believe Odette had ever existed. I had come to Venice once more, hoping that the city would awaken her within me, and on the hotel's terrace, as Aunt Foufy's voice rose and fell like the wavelets of the lagoon, there were moments when I felt as if something I had long struggled to remember was about to break unfettered into the forefront of my mind—but no matter how near it seemed, the memory would never materialize. Yet my mother's touch, her smile, and the sound of her voice seemed so close, so very close, that I felt compelled to pursue the past that eluded me. This is why I had welcomed the news that Uncle Leo's cousin Esther, who lived in the ghetto, had known Odette fairly well. Though Esther could be odd, even a little touched, Uncle Leo said, he thought it worth our while to pay her a visit. Esther had told him that she would be glad to meet us the next morning at her place in the Casa di Riposo, the ghetto's home for the aged.

I stood by the vaporetto's railing gazing at the black lagoon when the belfry tower of San Servolo's convent appeared silhouetted against the moonlit sky. The same tower appears in Shelley's poem "Julian and Madalo," black against the fading sun. San Servolo was then a madhouse, and the sight of the belfry tower has Julian rave against the Christian belief that madmen should pray to a god who made them mad. It is in San Servolo that Julian and Madalo meet the Maniac, who suffered the torments of disappointed love from which Julian wished he could cure him:

> But I imagined that if day by day
> I watched him, and but seldom went away,
> And studied all the beatings of his heart
> With zeal, as men study some stubborn art
> For their own good, and could patience find
> An entrance to the caverns of his mind,
> I might reclaim him from his dark estate.

The lines I thought long forgotten flowed into my head, I don't know where from, and the idea that if I strove to enter the caverns of my mind, I too might reclaim my own past from its dark estate, momentarily brushed my doubts away and cheered me up. The vaporetto hummed on toward San Marco, and what I saw as we approached the piazza struck me as a good omen. The Ducal Palace, over which hung a smiling moon, greeted me with all lights ablaze. Venice had put on her tiara and thrown a party for me.

The following day, after an early lunch, a water taxi drove me through a tangle of side canals to the Ponte delle Guglie at the entrance to the Ghetto Vecchio. I knew where I was only after the motor launch crossed the Grand Canal and San Geremia's belfry tower came into view, and only when the boat pulled up by the vaporetto stop did I realize that, immured in my mind, I had been completely oblivious of my surroundings. I paid the driver and walked to Rio Terà di San Leonardo, the wide and busy street that leads to the ghetto's oldest entrance. The oldest part of the ghetto, misleadingly called Ghetto Nuovo, is a small island ringed by unusually tall buildings with a large courtyard at its center. The wall of buildings is in turn encircled by canals, like a castle by its moat, and the old wooden bridge that leads though a passageway into the ghetto, the bridge I intended to cross, reminds one of a drawbridge. Carved into the wall of buildings, the dark passageway was in the 1500s locked by a heavy wooden gate that caged Venetian Jews inside the ghetto. When the Marangona rang the end of the working day, Christian guards closed the gate, only to reopen it when the bell rang again at sunrise. The Council of Ten wished to restrict contact, especially of a sexual nature, between Jews and Christians to the necessary minimum. Only Jewish physicians, singers, and dancers, and a few select merchants, were allowed to leave the ghetto after hours.

As any Venetian Jew will tell you with a curious mixture of anger and pride, the small island was named after the foundry that had once operated there. The Italian word for foundry is *geto*—and so it was that in a purely accidental way the segregation of the Jews of Venice marred this perfectly innocent word with its modern meaning. For almost three centuries Jews were gated in the ghetto and forced to identify themselves by wearing the yellow hat that replaced the yellow badge they once had to sew on their shirts. Subject to a variety of restrictions on the trades they could practice, Jews were mostly confined to a few pecuniary activities. German and Italian Jews traded in pawned goods and secondhand clothing while Levantine Jews, due to their extensive networks in the Ottoman world, were allowed an important role in international commerce. Despite the hardships and checkered relations between Jews and Venetian authorities, the Jews fared relatively well, much better than they did in the twentieth century when, between 1943 and 1944, two hundred of them were sent to extermination camps, as everyone emerging from the dark passageway into the bright square, like I now was, is almost immediately reminded. The brick wall at the far end of the Campo del Ghetto Nuovo is studded with bronze plaques depicting scenes from the Holocaust. Walking toward it, I saw a man with graying hair in a blue shirt and a petite woman in a beige dress looking at the memorial plaques. As they turned in the direction of the Casa di Reposo I realized they were my aunt and uncle. They stopped by the home's arched door and waved when they saw me coming.

Esther's musty room was on the first floor. A lively woman in her late seventies, she greeted us with a restrained smile that revealed a touch of ironic amusement, or so I thought when she lifted her eyes from the television set and raised a finger to her lips indicating that we could come in as long as we refrained from interrupting. Esther sat in an overstuffed armchair, her metal cane leaning on the fraying armrest. Books and newspapers were piled against the walls and on the table. Aunt Foufy sat on the chair next to Esther's while Uncle Leo crossed the room and sat on the bed. Sliding onto a wooden chair next to the door, I turned toward the television screen. Esther was watching an old black-and-white movie I recognized as *Dinner at Eight*, one of my favorites, and I understood why she had shushed us. The movie was nearing its end, and the scene now unfurling before us was one of the best. Kitty Packard (Jean Harlow), the lascivious wife of a bullying millionaire, is walking with Carlotta Vance (Marie Dressler), a washed-up diva with a wry wit, toward the dining room of an elegantly appointed house. "I was reading a book the other day," Kitty says. Carlotta raises her eyebrows mockingly, as if amazed by the very idea that Kitty may have read a book. "It's a screwy sort of book," Kitty continues, "all about the future. This man thinks that someday machines will take the place of every known profession." Carlota then looks sultry Kitty up and down and says, "That, my dear, is something you need never worry about."

Esther laughed quietly and, pointing the remote control at the television, turned it off. It was then that I noticed on the wall above her a canvas copy of Jacques Louis David's portrait of Napoleon in which, his cape flying in the wind, the future emperor rides his rearing white steed before the rising wall of the Alps. Thanks to my father, David's painting, as well as Napoleon himself, had featured prominently in my early teens. My father had given me a hefty volume on Napoleon, the dust jacket of which bore a glossy reproduction of the painting that hung on Esther's wall. I had spent years of my tender youth fired up by the book's glorious images of the great Corsican and his battles. Then one day I discovered that he had crossed the Alps on a disappointing mule. As I sat in Esther's room, mystified by the presence of David's painting, I wondered whether Uncle Leo's cousin knew of the unacknowledged beast of burden that had dutifully carried the chubby Corsican over the mountains.

"I can see you are Albert's son," Esther said. "You look just like your father." Uncle Leo nodded and asked her how she had been since he had last seen her. Pointing at her swollen legs, Esther told him she was fine but her legs weren't. She explained how difficult it was to get around Venice as one aged. "There are no minivans," she said, "to transport the old from door to door. There are boats, of course, but you have to walk to get one; there is no other way." Uncle Leo made a gesture of protest and was about to say something when Esther quickly stopped him. "I know, I know," she moaned, "but I don't want to go live with you in Milan. You help me enough as it is, Leo, and you know how grateful I am. You and Foufy are my angels, but I want to stay here in the ghetto where Marco died. He's buried in Venice, and I cannot leave him. Don't worry; people take care of me here. There is a kind man who works at the Jewish Museum who visits me regularly, and he takes me to the synagogue every Friday. I go to the Scuola Levantina in the Ghetto Vecchio, and I'll keep going there as long as I can walk. You've been there, haven't you? The baroque carvings of the wooden *tebah* are gorgeous. So are the golden chandeliers and the marble ark. The synagogues in Venice are so intimate, with their red curtains and all that gold, like a room in a baroque palace. They are so special. I hate that women are still separated from the men. We sit in the upstairs gallery behind wooden grilles, like women used to sit behind *mushrabiya* screens in harems. It's ridiculous and it also means that I have to go up another flight of stairs. But what can I do?"

Aunt Foufy slid a large box of Perugino chocolates onto Esther's lap, and the older woman blew her a kiss. "You spoil me," she said, and tearing away the cellophane wrap, she opened the box and passed it around. As the box reached me I picked a nugget of gianduia and began to open its golden wrap. Esther chuckled. "It took chocolate," she said, "to move your eyes away from my Napoleon, eh?" She spoke in a perfect French accent. I imagined that like my father she must have spent some time in France weaning herself of the heavy French accent of Levantine

53

Jews. The painting also told me that like my father and many other Egyptian Jews, most of whom had gone through the mill of French colonial schools, Esther must be a lover of things French, a Francophile of the first order. But there were other reasons for Esther's unbridled veneration of Napoleon.

"This painting here," Esther said, "has caused me a lot of trouble. Venetians, who are a very peculiar breed of people, hate Napoleon because he brought their glorious republic to its knees, and he was only twenty-eight, mind you, when he did so. They blame him for the final decay of Venice. Nonsense. *La Serenissima*, as it is called for some silly reason, had been going downhill for a few centuries before Napoleon paid it any attention. Venetians forget that they brought their demise upon themselves. Napoleon gave them every opportunity to side with him, or at least to remain neutral, but the Venetian oligarchy preferred the reactionary Austrians. They sided with obscurantism. They didn't want to embrace the ideals of the French Revolution. They clung to the retrograde values of the most conservative empire in Europe. Napoleon gave the Venetians a chance, and what did they do? They let the Austrian troops cross Venetian territory to occupy the town of Pescheria. Napoleon was furious. He threatened to burn Verona to the ground if the Venetians refused to let his troops into the city. Even so, he offered Venetians a second chance to side with the French. But the aristocrats in the Doge's Palace turned up their noses and refused. So when the commander of the Lido fortress opened fire on a harmless French ship and killed its crew, instead of punishing the stupid commander, Venetian rulers congratulated him. Is it any wonder that Napoleon then swore to become Venice's Attila? Is it any mystery that he should remove the winged lion of San Marco from its column and ship it to Paris with the four bronze horses from the Basilica?" Esther looked inquisitively around the room and then relaxed into a soft chuckle.

"As for me," she said with a grin, "I'll always worship Napoleon no matter what they say. It's true that he razed many churches to the ground and stole paintings and other valuable things from

Venice. But we must not forget the great things he did. Every Jew is indebted to Napoleon because he was the first one to have the courage to tear down ghetto walls throughout Europe, including those of the Ghetto Nuovo. Lafayette's *Declaration of the Rights of Man* is a fine piece of writing, as you know, but it took a man like Napoleon to get things done." At this point I almost protested that Napoleon wasn't as good as all that. It was well known that the slave trade had flourished under his auspices, and there were other things about Napoleon I could have said, but, as usual, I held my tongue.

Out of words, Esther was now training her eagle eyes on us, searching for any reaction she might feed on to continue her diatribe. As no one in the room seemed in the mood to argue, Esther slumped back in her velvet armchair. Uncle Leo gazed at me, at once proud of his cousin's obvious intellectual gifts and embarrassed by her equally noticeable weakness for interminable rants. Uneasy as he was, though, Uncle Leo refused any responsibility for his cousin's eccentricities. With a slight shrug of his shoulders he signaled his helplessness and exempted himself of all culpability. For my part, taken as I was by the old woman's verve, I was even more intrigued by how much I had forgotten of what my father had once told me about Napoleon. Only after Esther had spoken did I recall my father's lectures on the great man as an enlightened protector of the Jews. I suppose my father spoke so much about Jewish law, tradition, history, customs, lore, personalities, folktales, rituals, and prayers that my overwhelmed consciousness could not contain it all. My father's Jewishness had run over the top layers of my memory and spilled into deeper crevices, where it hid until Esther's rant brought it back bubbling to the surface of my mind. My father's frowning face suddenly loomed in the amber light of some forgotten room, and his ponderous lecturing filled me with complicated ambivalences.

Meanwhile, Esther was addressing me in a soothing voice. "When Leo told me," she said, "that you were coming to see me, I was amazed by how strange life is. I met your mother years before you were born. It must have been shortly before the war started, in the late thirties. She was part of a group of five or six young women I frequented. We were seventeen or eighteen years old at the time, daughters of well-off families that frequented the Gezira Sporting Club in Zamalek. You remember the club, don't you? I wasn't her best friend. Nadine was. Nadine was prettier than Elizabeth Taylor, and she and Odette were the leaders of the pack. Odette wasn't beautiful in the conventional sense, but she was tall and striking. She looked like a flamenco dancer. She and Nadine were both very articulate, very funny, and popular with the boys; all girls wanted to be friends with them. As I'm sure you can see, even then I wasn't the prettiest thing standing on two legs—and I liked books a little too much. I fancied myself superior to the other girls, and, as you can imagine, they retaliated by making fun of me. Except for Odette. She could have a sharp tongue, but she was kind and helped others without making too much of a fuss. The other girls teased me about my glasses, my bookishness, my awkwardness, but she never did, and when they wouldn't stop and I'd get angry, because, you know, I was no doormat either, she would grab me by the arm and whisk me away. 'They're silly,' she'd say. 'They have nothing in their little heads.' Not that she was any intellectual. She wasn't. But she had some appreciation for the things of the mind and liked to hear me talk as long as I explained myself clearly. Otherwise she'd complain that I was boring her. Odette gave you the impression that she hadn't a care in the world, always appearing joyful, with a ready smile on her lips. She smiled with her whole face, an infectious smile that could disarm a Panzer. I think she was basically a happy person, but she had a sad, brooding side she hid from others.

"I remember—it's strange how we remember things so vividly, or at least we imagine we do. I remember Odette sitting alone on a bench under a big tree at the end of a lawn. I walked across the lawn toward her, and when she saw me coming she greeted me with a smile. I could see that there was something wrong, and I asked her what was the matter. She pretended she was surprised and raised her eyebrows like people do when they pretend they don't know what you are talking about. But when I sat beside her and insisted she tell me, her face turned somber, and I thought she was going to cry. 'I adore my parents,' she said, 'but they are not being reasonable lately.' I remember the word she used— *reasonable*—because it struck me as odd for a young woman to talk like this about her parents. 'They quarrel all the time,' she complained, 'and my father, who is usually a sweet man, is now throwing tantrums.' *Crise de nerfs* is the expression she used to describe her father's tantrums. 'My father,' Odette continued, with a tear rolling down her cheek, 'isn't treating my mother as he should; he should be nicer to her. She is a beautiful woman, a devoted wife, and a wonderful mother. What else does he want? For the past two or three months, my father has been coming home later. Late at night they have these awful scenes behind the closed doors of their bedroom. They think I'm sleeping, but I'm wide awake, and I can hear their angry whispers.'

"I did my best," Esther said, "to comfort her, suspecting all along what I'm sure Odette had already sensed: that her father, your grandfather Gad, was having an affair. But she was too reserved a person to allow herself any further confidences.

"That sunny afternoon, facing the lawn in the shade of the tree, we got as close to each other as we would ever get. Not much later I met Marco, my husband, and after that I saw little of Odette and the other girls. There was also, I'm sorry to say, the fact that I never liked Albert, your father. The funny thing is that Leo and I are from Corfu, and we are relatives of Albert Cohen, the writer, and I don't like him much either. He wrote *Solal*, a very boring novel. His other novels are boring too. Anyhow, Albert, your father, was in my opinion a bit too pretentious and authoritarian. He thought he was God's gift, if not to the world, certainly to women." (At this Uncle Leo chuckled with glee, amused, I'm sure, by the old lady's zing, but also, I suspect, because he was of the same opinion regarding my father's character.)

"In Albert's presence," Esther continued, "Odette became another person. She acted like a little girl doing her utmost to please her father. It was 'Albert, my darling' and 'your little woman loves you so' all the time, and he sat there letting her pamper him like a pasha. I never liked this kind of thing, and I was never good at hiding what I felt, so, as you can imagine, we drifted apart, and I wasn't invited to her wedding. They were married in the main downtown synagogue, the Adly Temple, and Nadine told me it was a grand affair, with the chief rabbi officiating and many important people present. I was angry and didn't invite them to my wedding either. Although we weren't on speaking terms for a while, Odette was so good-natured that she and I made peace and ended up having a good laugh at the whole thing. We didn't see much of each other until one day Nadine told me Odette had fallen gravely ill. Nadine and I went to see her at the hospital."

Esther put her gnarled fingers over her mouth, visibly shaken by the image she had conjured up in her mind. Watching how much distress the distant memory of my sick mother had caused her, my heart gnarled as badly as her fingers. "Poor Odette," Esther finally said, "she sat on the hospital bed propped up by pillows. She was as white as the pillows against which she reclined. She looked exhausted, at the end of her tether. There was a horrible smell of disinfectant in the room. When we asked why she didn't lie down and rest, she said she couldn't breathe well. 'I'm afraid I will die if I lie down,' she said. I remember her words as if she had spoken them a minute ago."

It was almost three o'clock when Aunt Foufy told us she was tired and wished to return to the hotel. After I hugged Esther and thanked her, I walked with Aunt Foufy and Uncle Leo through the Ghetto Vecchio to the vaporetto stop, where we said our good-byes and promised each other we would stay in touch. I waved until the boat vanished behind its wake, then crossed the Ponte delle Guglie to Campo San Geremia and walked down Rio Terrà Lista de Spagna toward the Ponte dei Scalzi, where I crossed to Santa Croce. I missed Foufy, Leo, and Esther, and, wanting to distract my heavy heart, I gave myself something to do, a destination: I would visit the Scuola di San Rocco. Tintoretto had spent two decades of his life decorating the confraternity with more than fifty paintings. I had seen several pictures of his *Annunciation*, never the original, but I remembered it well. The vigor with which the archangel Gabriel and a battalion of cherubs charge through Mary's doorless house, rare among the paintings of this kind, effectively conveys the shock imparted by the news the startled virgin is about to receive. I focused on the painting, my mind evoking one detail or another as I walked down the Calle del Oglio, but the painting's seductions could not hold my attention for long. Soon I found my thoughts drifting back to what had transpired in Esther's room. Uncle Leo's chuckle resounded in my ears, and now, in retrospect, I could hear a note of mockery in his laughter. It seemed to me that I had mistaken a snicker for a chuckle. Perhaps my mother had confided secrets to Uncle Leo that had indisposed him toward my father.

Odette had been staying at Leo and Foufy's cramped apartment for more than a month when complaints about my father's repeated postponements of his arrival began to appear in her letters to him. "So now," she writes on May 29, 1952, "you are apparently arriving only on the twenty-second of June according to Victor. Why so late, *cheri*? You said the first in your last letter. I don't understand any of this; please write and let me know the exact date on which you plan to arrive. Make it the earliest possible, please. I no longer want to rot in Milan. I've had enough. The weather has been horrible; it rains constantly. My old bones make me suffer; this rheumatism is poison." On June 2, Odette is sad to learn that my father will, in fact, embark only on the twenty-second. "I was very sad," she writes, "to hear through Isabelle that you will leave on the twenty-second. One more month. Ouf! My God, it will be a long time. Well, if your work demands your presence, there is nothing to be done. Darling, I know I'm repeating myself, but I can't help it; I miss you terribly. I am eager to have you by my side. I talk about you all the time, at home, in town, during our excursions outside the city; everyone thinks I adore you, and you know it's true." On June 9, upon hearing that my father will embark only in July, her annoyance borders on exasperation: "I'm getting tired of waiting for you. I've been here for too long already. I have now been at Foufy's for two months. I feel ashamed. And now you tell me you are coming only in the middle of July?" Two weeks later her impatience thickens: "I can't wait to go to Venice. Should I take my own and the children's luggage with me, or will we come back here before we leave for Egypt? Is your ship still the *Esperia*? Or are you taking another one. When exactly will you be arriving in Venice?"

In the few letters Odette sent to her mother, Marie, she reveals deeper resentments. The fawning and submissiveness Esther begrudged her may have been an act, the price of a relationship with my father, which in the beginning must have seemed trivial but grew onerous with time. In her most revealing letter to her mother Odette relates an insight she had during a dinner Leo's older brother hosted for the family. "I was invited to dinner at the Battinos," she writes, "and they were full of compliments. I must have made an impression. An uncle of Leo's from America asked me if he could sculpt my bust. I couldn't believe I still had that kind of power. I think Albert took away all personality I may have had with his tyrannical ways. But all of this will change. You'll see."

My mother did not live long enough to follow through with her threats, but I suppose these were in any case idle, the idle threats of a woman who was raised to be a housewife. Feeling angry and dejected in Milan, and not getting much attention from Foufy, my mother must have turned to Uncle Leo for comfort. Odette's letters are full of praise for him, especially as a tender and loving husband, praise that, genuine as it may have been, also carried a veiled criticism of my father's neglect. Uncle Leo's comments about my father's excess of testosterone (his alleged aping of Tarzan), as well as his chuckle following Esther's derisive comments, suggested that he must have taken her side against my father. But there was more to Uncle Leo's attitude toward my father.

Although I cannot say which feature of Uncle Leo's face gave the malice away, the malice had been unmistakably there. I could swear he suspected that my father had delayed his trip to Europe for reasons other than work, and, oddly enough, this suspicion found its reflection in my mother's expressed insecurities about my father's faithfulness. In most of the thirteen letters she wrote to my father, Odette warns him not to be unfaithful to her. On May 5 she writes: "You swear that you love me and that you are faithful to me. You better be, because if you dare, I am sure I'll do the same. So be careful. You are forewarned." On May 20 she is uncertain: "Is it your work, your clinic, that keeps you so busy? Are you sure?" On May 22, she threatens: "I assume there is no pretty blonde underneath all this. Careful with infidelities. There are many handsome men in Italy, and there is hot Spanish blood in my veins, and I know how to take revenge, don't I?" This goes on, letter after letter, the threats subsiding only as my father sets the final date of arrival. Then they are replaced with frantic preparations for her trip to Venice, where she will wait for him, and they are to go to an unnamed hotel on the Lido.

I imagined Odette watching the handsome *Esperia* gliding into the lagoon, at once exhilarated by the thought of seeing the man she loved and frightened by the prospect of being trapped with him in an unhappy marriage. I imagined my mother, alone on the Piazetta, hearing the loud moan of the *Esperia*'s foghorn rising like a lament from the sea, and I wondered if she felt the same anguish I do upon hearing the sound that in me unfailingly evokes the melancholy of exile.

I fully intended to visit the confraternity of San Rocco, but upon reaching the entrance I was overcome by a sense of futility that sapped my will to go inside. Mollified by a lassitude that numbed my limbs, I thought it better to sit on the shallow steps of the scuola and watch the tide of people come and go. The thought that the dramatic upheavals of my parent's lives, their fears and hopes, would vanish without a trace made all motion pointless. My body and soul wished for the brute oblivion of an open-jawed reptile baking in the sun. So strong was my wish that I would no doubt have fallen asleep had it not been for the sudden appearance of a dark-haired man who bore a striking resemblance to my father. He walked close to the huge brick wall of the Frari church, a dignified figure I could not mistake for anyone else.

The sight of my father jolted me back into the far past, and though I knew it futile to pursue him, an irresistible curiosity had me jump to my feet and follow him. At the end of the wall he turned left toward the gabled entrance of the Gothic church and disappeared. Reaching the entrance a few minutes later, I stepped into the vast interior and caught a glimpse of a white-clad man just before he vanished behind the elaborate carvings of the rood screen that fenced the monk's choir and the altar beyond it. I hurried to the screen and entered the choir but saw only a nun dressed in white. I searched for my father everywhere until, forlorn of all hope, I raised my eyes upwards and, awestruck, realized I was before Titian's *Assunta*.

On a massive billowing cloud, Mary soared toward God in a whirlwind of winged cherubs. Below her, the earthbound apostles raised their heads in awe as Mary ascended in the golden light of heaven. One of the apostles arched his back and stretched out his arm as if to catch the cloud. I pitied him, and I pitied myself, and earthbound like he was, I too wished I could catch the cloud and ascend with the Virgin Mother into the resplendent light of heaven.

III

Butantã, São Paulo

Praça do Patriarca, a square in the old center of São Paulo, honors José Bonifácio de Andrade e Silva, the patriarch of Brazilian independence. When I think of Praça Patriarca, I remember another patriarch, my own father, who for years worked in a building a stone's throw away from the square. On this crisp September morning in 1998 it was he, as usual, who sprung to mind as I strolled under the hypermodern structure recently erected over the square as a sort of triumphal arch that, metallic and ungainly, grimly foreshadows the coming annihilation of the old center. Around this arch, garlanded façades, mansard roofs, fanciful turrets, and lacy balconies survive in a sooty state of disrepair. Their splendor is gone, but they still have the power to evoke the old-world charms of nineteenth century São Paulo.

Ambling down the bustling streets behind the square, I conjured up the coffee shops I used to frequent with my father. His favorite was a small café on Rua Direita, where we ate a delicious *queijo na chapa*, a grilled cheese sandwich that exuded a heavenly smell.

Rua Direita and two other streets form a triangle next to the patriarch's square and sit atop a hill known as the Old City. This is where the city began. At the edge of the square the hill slopes down into the Valley of Anhangabaú. Half a mile away, on the other side of the valley, rises another hill, called Morro do Chá, once the site of Indian tea plantations. In the latter part of the nineteenth century, when coffee plantations made their owners fabulously wealthy, the two hills were joined by the Viaduto do Chá, or Tea Viaduct, an eight-hundred-foot iron bridge imported from Germany that stretched over the Valley of Anhangabaú.

From Praça Patriarca one could take a tram across the viaduct to the Teatro Municipal, a theatre modeled on the Paris Opéra that rose magnificent above the valley. Beyond the theatre, in the streets that lead to leafy Praça da República, jazzy art deco buildings once mingled with the ornate Belle Époque style of the older edifices. In the early seventies, just before I left, although the growing number of cars had begun to take its toll, it still was a pleasure to walk along the tree-lined streets of the city.

I know São Paulo is no longer what it then was, that the center is now dirty and run down, its buildings crumbling from neglect, and though my mind cannot deny the bitter truth, my eyes see only the beauty of the past in the ruins of the present. On that brilliant winter day, when I crossed the viaduct and stood facing the Teatro Municipal, I had eyes only for the majestic façade of my boyhood.

The theatre's marble columns and allegorical sculptures thrilled me as they had when I first climbed its stairs with my father and stepmother to see *Aida*. My stepmother Liz and I, often at odds with each other, must have been on good terms that day. She had patiently told me Aida's story beforehand. Adding flourishes of her own, Liz explained how the great pharaohs had been entombed in the pyramids. She described what seemed to me a complicated mechanism whereby large quantities of sand kept huge blocks of stone from sealing the entrance to the burial chamber. When released, the sand freed the massive blocks to slam shut and seal the chamber containing the pharaoh's sarcophagus and his panicked entourage. "And this is how," Liz had said, "Radames and Aida were buried alive in the crypt of the Temple of Vulcan. This is why they sing, 'The fatal stone now closes over me.'" Standing before the theatre I recalled the fear and excitement with which I heard Liz's account. No matter how difficult a person she was, Liz was always interesting. I was glad, though not entirely free from ambivalence, to have an opportunity to see her again.

I had postponed my trip to Cairo and come from Venice to São Paulo upon hearing from my brother Pierre that Liz had been hospitalized after fainting on the street. There had been the possibility of a stroke, but this turned out to be a false alarm, and she was now at home less than a half an hour walk from the Teatro Municipal. Liz inhabited the same small two-bedroom apartment she had moved to with my half brothers after divorcing my father. Liz's apartment is not far from Rua Fortunato, the street on which we had all lived during the years our family lasted. We lived at one end of the street, and my maternal grandparents, who arrived from Cairo two years later, at the other, and it was on this not so fortunate Rua Fortunato that the drama of my teen years unfolded.

My sister and I first met Liz in Paris, where we spent the Christmas season before embarking on the Italian liner that took us to Brazil. We had much fun walking in the drizzle along the glistening, festive boulevards, stopping here and there in a warm café for a hot chocolate and a creamy napoleon. I liked Liz then and was happy when she later joined us in Brazil. She introduced me to exciting books and talked about things nobody had before. My father had little time to do so, and my grandparents, adoring as they were, knew little about books. Liz and I spent entire afternoons reading poetry and looking at color reproductions of paintings in oversized books. She had a predilection for Italian poets, especially the Tuscan poet Giosué Carducci, and she also loved Cavafy, the Greek poet from Alexandria. There were a handful of poems she recited often, like "Pianto Antico" and "Voices," mournful poems she read with great feeling. The two last stanzas of "Pianto Antico," which lament the death of Carducci's infant son, were her favorite:

Tu fior della mia pianta
percossa e inaridita,
tu de l'inutil vita
estremo unico fior,

sei nela terra freda,
sei nela terra negra;
nè il sol più ti rallegra
nè ti risveglia amor.

Liz was as fluent in Italian and English as she was in French because her mother, Rosetta, came from Trieste and her father, Captain Vivian Cesar David Levy, a Jew of Maltese origin, was an Englishman and an officer in the British army. She had a weakness for English, and later she taught at the Cultura Inglesa of São Paulo, where I continued to study the language, as she did not want me to forget the little I had learned at the Gezira Preparatory School.

Walking along Rua Barão de Itapetininga, the thoroughfare that connects the Viaduto do Chá to Praça da República, I thought with regret about my stepmother, about the turbulent years that followed our descent into mutual acrimony. I threaded my way through the horde of human ads, the poor souls that crowd the center of the city wearing advertising placards like wooden ponchos, brooding over the slow disintegration of my family. Slowly, sadly, the family had fallen apart at the melancholy pace of the bossa nova. Less than a year after "The Girl from Ipanema" appeared in the famous Getz/Gilberto album of 1964, my stepmother and two small brothers had moved out to the apartment she still lives in, and I had moved in with my grandparents. Only my father and sister had stayed at Rua Fortunato, in the apartment the six of us had shared.

As I looked in vain for the Librairie Larousse, the bookstore in a gallery of Barão de Itapetininga where my father had bought me the slick tome on Napoleon, it struck me that the half-baked explanations now part of the family lore never rose beyond the pedestrian level of recrimination. Looking back, it seemed that my grandparents, my father, my sister, and I, governed by some treacherous law of life, lived out a version of the archetypal fable of the wicked stepmother. My mother's premature death had turned her into a saint, and her perfection, unmatchable because untried, had imprisoned us in a cramped cell in which every little grudge acquired calamitous proportions. If Liz would so much as ask me to wash the dishes, I would march to my grandparents' apartment and add this fact to a long list of grievances. Armed with the ammunition I gave him, my grandfather would then confront my father, who, caught between the conflicting demands of his wife, in-laws, and son, not to speak of his own mercurial nature, would lose his temper and gain in this way the enmity of all parties concerned. In time my father came to embody the bullying tyrant, my stepmother the wicked witch, and we, my sister and I, the innocent victims whose only protectors were my heroic grandparents. In retrospect, this wasteful war of all against all seems ludicrous, a compounding of trifle misunderstandings that a pinch of wisdom might have easily avoided. But wisdom is seldom available when most needed. In the heat of the moment all the damage we cause others easily finds its justification, or so I glumly thought, as I opened the wooden door to the diminutive Otis elevator that would take me to my stepmother's apartment.

Liz greeted me with a rousing fanfare. While we had never regained the intimacy of earlier days, she and I, to my father's chagrin, had nevertheless agreed to an armistice. We made a concerted effort to stay on good terms, if for nothing else, at least to preserve the affection among my brothers and me. We sat on the sofa of her living room, amid a profusion of pillows and paisley shawls, facing a huge color photograph of a narrow footpath among sycamore trees in autumn. Enamored of trees, Liz sketched them obsessively. She drew oaks with thin layers of snow on their twisted branches, firs in lofty alpine landscapes, and birches by brilliant silvery springs, and, unable to live among her beloved trees, she had brought them into her living room.

Liz looked up from behind her glasses. Would I like a Turkish coffee? I nodded and she called out to her maid to make *um café turco*. When Liz saw my gaze shift to *The Sufis*, a book that lay open, face down on the table, she said that old age had kindled in her a renewed interest in mysticism. "Besides," Liz continued, as if she needed further justification, "there are very funny stories in this little book. Idries Shad, the author, is a famous Indian-born sufi of Afghan origin who died a controversial figure. Some claim he was a Sayyed, a biological descendent of the Prophet Mohammed, while others think him an impostor.

"But never mind all this," Liz said, dismissing the controversy with a sweep of the hand. "The important thing is that he tells wonderful stories. The stories are meant to awaken people, but I find them delightful in their own right. There's one story in which Mullah Nasruddin, a legendary Sufi character, loads a donkey with straw and takes him across some border. He does this every day for many years. Since he has admitted to the border guards that he is a smuggler, they search his person and sift through the straw again and again, occasionally even burning it to find the precious merchandise, but find absolutely nothing. Meanwhile Nasrudin grows visibly richer with every passing year. Many years later, after Nasrudin retires, one of the customs officials meets him in another country and asks him to reveal what he had been smuggling and why he had never been caught. And what do you think Nasrudin answered? Donkeys, of course—donkeys.

"Isn't this a good story?" Liz asked. "Its point is that we never see what's under our noses, but it's a delightful way of saying it, don't you think? To tell the truth, I'm reading mystics because I'm scared. Fainting like I did in the middle of the street gave me the scare of my life. I regained consciousness fairly quickly but I couldn't stand up. There was something wrong with my balance, something that had me swaying from side to side like a drunk. If it weren't for a kind man who drove me to the hospital, I don't know what would have become of me. Thank God the doctors at the Einstein Hospital, the very best in the city, found no evidence of a stroke. They put my head in one of those awful machines and took those fancy X-rays, but they couldn't find anything. They now think there's a problem with my inner ear. I feel much better, but I've been put on notice. My weight has to come down. I don't know if I can give up my beer and my cheese and my olives and my french fries, but I'll try."

The maid came into the room in a flowery cotton dress and flip-flops and set down on the table a tray with a pot of coffee, a sugar bowl, and cups and saucers. The Turkish coffee pot looked like the one my father had bought in Cairo at Khan el Khalili. Liz poured the thick brew, which, as it slowly slid down the pot's beak, filled the room with the aroma of cardamom and coffee. "Pierre tells me," she said, "that you wanted some photographs of my first husband, Ralph. I found only a few good ones. Looking at the photographs brought back a mixed bag of good and not-so-good memories of Egypt. Ralph was a scoundrel. He was a pilot in the Royal Air Force who came to Cairo with thousands of British troops. When the war broke out, you couldn't go anywhere in the city without seeing an English soldier. They were everywhere, in their khaki uniforms and their knee-length shorts. They filled the cafés and nightclubs, and especially the Birka, a long street north of the Ezbekiyya Gardens that led to the sleazy brothels of Cairo.

"I met Ralph at the pool of the Gezira Sporting Club. Ralph approached me with strands of blond hair licking his brow, and I fell for his raffish charm even though I knew somewhere in the back of my mind that this was a mistake. My father and Ralph were birds of a feather and they took to each other instantly. My mother liked him too. So we got married. It wasn't long before Ralph came home late and drunk and smelling of cheap perfume. I put up with him because it was fun to be around him. Well—I don't really know why I did put up with Ralph. I traveled all over North Africa with him, following him wherever he was stationed, and it was an exciting adventure for an inexperienced young woman like I was. One day I caught him with another woman in my own bed. That did it. We were living in Tunisia in a white house, and for some reason I came back from an errand an hour or so before I was supposed to, and there he was, his hairy bottom bobbing up and down between her thighs."

Liz shrugged her shoulders and took another sip of coffee. "Those RAF pilots were all the same. Boozers and womanizers. They were scared, I suppose. Ralph fought at El Alamein. He was a highly decorated pilot. He was stationed at Burg el Arab, a tiny village thirty miles from Alexandria, midway between Alamein and the city. I'm sure you must know of it because it appears in Durell's *Alexandria Quartet* as the site where Nessim Hosnani builds a summer palace for his wife, Justine. There is a lovely passage in *Justine* where Nessim sees an Arab fort among the white dunes of a deserted beach. He watches the waves crashing against the shore and imagines the miniature oasis of palm and fig trees where he will build a summer palace for his wife. The fort Durrell mentions was in reality a carpet factory. The British built it in Burg el Arab for the Bedouin widows whose husbands had been killed in the first war. Egyptian nationalists closed the place down, but in the thirties the government allowed Judge Brinton and his circle to build weekend houses close to the carpet factory. I remember reading somewhere that Durrell learned about Burg el Arab and the geography of Mareotis in a book written by Cosson, who was a relative of the factory's builder.

"Ralph went to Burg el Arab, and from there he flew many missions against Rommel's Afrika Corps. He was there for First and Second Alamein, for the whole bloody carnage. Thousands of men died in the desert. Soldiers from all over the world, from England, Australia, New Zealand, India, Greece, France, Italy, Germany, are buried there. Miles of little white crosses cover the desert around Alamein. Were it not for Montgomery and these young soldiers and pilots, Rommel would have taken Egypt, and it would have been the end of civilization as we know it. The Suez Canal was the vital route through which the Allies brought oil to Europe, and Churchill had to keep Rommel from taking Egypt. Churchill visited Burg el Arab when Ralph was there. I think it was after First Alamein; he went there to put some pressure on Montgomery. Ralph told me that Churchill went for a swim in the sea, and when someone raised his camera to take a picture he stuck his arm out of the water and made the victory sign. I never saw or met Churchill in Alexandria, though I had friends who did, but Ralph introduced me to Maskelyne."

When Liz mentioned Maskelyne I was puzzled because she talked about him as if he were a real person, and I remembered him as a fictional character in Durell's novel *Mountolive*. In the novel Maskelyne is a lean intelligence brigadier with a leathery face who smokes a pipe and uncovers, to Ambassador Mountolive's dismay, the Coptic plot led by Nessim Hosnani. For a moment I thought Liz had, in fact, suffered a stroke, conferring life as she was to a fictional character, and my befuddlement must have shown because she immediately set me right.

"No, no," she said. "Not *that* Maskelyne. Not the one from the *Alexandria Quartet*. Durrell used the name because it had become a symbol of deception, and he felt that deception was the hallmark of Alexandria. There was a real Maskelyne, who was an illusionist famous before the war for his levitation act. Apparently he managed to float the body of a hypnotized woman above the audience. This Maskelyne, the real one, was assigned to the Camouflage Corps in Egypt. His job was to disguise tanks into trucks.

"Montgomery wanted to deceive the Germans into thinking that a massive attack would come from the south, while he was, in fact, planning to attack them from the north. Maskelyne built dummy tanks made of wooden frames and sent them on jeeps to the south. Meanwhile he moved the real tanks disguised as supply lorries to the north, and that's how Montgomery defeated Rommel. Maskelyne's tricks made him famous in Alexandria. 'To do a Maskelyne' became a synonym for cheating, swindling, and bamboozling people. That's why Durrell called his shadowy character Maskelyne. He used him as a symbol of Alexandria. Durrell saw Alexandria as a city where people traded on illusion and false identities, a city in which things never were what they seemed.

"I met Jaspers Maskelyne sometime in 1942 at the Maison Baudrot, a fashionable café on Rue Fouad across the street from the British Information Office. Durrell too frequented Baudrot, by the way. He was put in charge of the office at about that time, and I saw him often at Baudrot, Pastroudis, and other cafés. Durrell was very short, almost a dwarf, but he seemed to hold everyone's attention—a dwarfish king holding court. I knew Durrell was short before I ever saw him, so I wasn't surprised when

I actually did. But Maskelyne was nothing like I had imagined him. In photographs taken before the war he looked like your stereotypical magician, like Mandrake, a dark man with a thin moustache, hypnotic eyes, and greased-up hair. When I met him he looked nothing like his old pictures. He looked disappointingly like your straight-laced British officer. Ralph and he and their friends got into a dull conversation, so I went home early and curled up in bed with a book. I'm sure Ralph and his buddies drank themselves into a stupor and ended up in one of the filthy brothels in the slums of the Arab quarter."

As Liz spoke, I again had that strange feeling that she was relating a scene from the *Alexandria Quartet*, the one in which Nessim and Darley look for Justine in a dark backyard of the Arab quarter. In the scene, the ululations of a burial procession pierce the night as the two men search for Justine in the dark alleys of the city. They finally reach the backyard, where, guided only by the flame of Nessim's lighter, they find Justine in a brothel among a dozen ten-year-old girls in nightgowns, their lips smeared with rouge. Nessim and Darley arrive just in time to rescue Justine, who is imprudently attacking a menacing sailor with a raised bottle in her hand.

"I married your father," Liz was now saying, "as a reaction to Ralph. Albert was everything Ralph wasn't. Albert was a solid family man, a man with whom I could have kids. He didn't come home drunk with lipstick on his neck. Unfortunately, Albert had many other problems. We like to think we have control over our lives, but we don't. We bounce from one thing to the next, reacting blindly to events, tossed this way and that by forces we barely understand. I went from Ralph to Albert, from one extreme to the other, as badly matched to the first husband as I was to the second. Ralph was all fun, and your father was no fun at all. He wanted me to fit his image of a respectable physician's wife. He wanted me to become *une femme comme il faut*. He urged me to change my wardrobe, to buy prudish dresses, and to stop smoking and drinking in public. He wanted me to attend services at the synagogue, to sit upstairs with the women. Can you imagine? And on top of everything your father was a miser. He never gave me enough money to run the house. He locked everything in that damn cupboard of his. You remember how he would give you a watch or a pen for your birthday, and then lock it away, saying he'd give it back to you in a few years? When you'd be more mature and responsible? Oh, well, I have no wish to complain about your father. Let's not get into this.

"I was talking about Ralph and Alexandria, about those years that were by far the most exciting of my life. This may be a cliché, but there is no other way of expressing it. Alexandria in those days was as cosmopolitan a city as you can imagine. It mixed the ancient and the modern, the European and the Oriental, in a way that was pure magic. You heard the muezzin's call to prayer while you drank a martini at the Cecil Hotel. There were Greek ruins, Turkish forts, minarets, French boulevards with swanky cafés, and the glorious Corniche. It was impossible not to fall in love with Alexandria. My mother loved Alexandria. Rosetta was her name, and Rue Fouad, the main street of the city, used to be called Rue Rosette. Rue de la Porte Rosette, actually. The street used to pass through a gate in the old Arab wall, and the gate was called Rosette. When my mother came to Alexandria she liked to take long walks in the Turkish town, along Rue Tatwig and Rue de France. She liked the small bazaars and the Terbana mosque. We would walk all the way up to Kait Bey Fort and walk back along the Corniche, watching the city's dark silhouette against the orange sky. We took our time, waiting for the sky to turn pink and blue while the city lights came on. The proximity of war enhanced the city's magic. The fear of annihilation gave the city a spice and a glow that held us all in a trance. During the second battle of Alamein the sky filled with fighters and bombers, and we could hear the thunder of guns in the distance and see the flashes light up the western sky. We stuck our ears to the radio, but the Germans had captured the transmitters, so all we could hear were messages to the German troops and the final 'Lili Marlene' song."

At this, my stepmother fell silent. She remained silent for a moment and then looked straight into my eyes. "I've been trying to say something to you," she said, "but I don't have the courage. That's why I've been talking about Ralph and Alexandria instead—beating around the bush. I want to apologize to you.

"You were just a boy," she said, and choked. She took my hand and squeezed it, and I, choking too, had an urge to make her laugh, to let her know in some way that I no longer held a grudge and felt as much regret as she did. "It's all right," I said, obviously in jest, "I forgive you." It took her two seconds to get over her surprise and break into a joyous, full-bodied laughter. "Let's have a beer," she said. "I have some Brahma, your favorite, and it's freezing cold, just the way you like it."

Liz went into the kitchen, and I had a sudden yearning for the hot summer nights I spent with my grandfather. He had given me my first taste of beer, which he poured into glass mugs he stored in his freezer. When I was a teen he allowed me to drink a few sips from his glass, usually when we played dominoes on the dining room table. I can still see the room in my mind. I see the line of black dominoes and their white dots on the lacy tablecloth. I see my grandfather frowning in concentration, and behind him my grandmother, her hand resting gently on his shoulder. Frozen in my memory, the moment is redolent of a joyful peace, a transcendent kind of beatitude I lamentably can no longer experience.

Two days after my visit with my stepmother, I came back to the center of the city, this time to visit Maurice Harrari, whom I had known for more than three decades. Maurice was in his midfifties, a quiet bachelor whose oddities had evolved into full-fledged eccentricities after his mother's death. Maurice had stayed in the roomy apartment he had once shared with his mother at Rua Cesário Motta Jr., only two buildings away from the apartment my father had lived in after he retired. Rua Cesário Motta was also near my grandfather's store on Largo do Arouche. In my teens I would often walk from home at Rua Fortunato to Rua Cesário Motta, spend the afternoon with Maurice, and in the early evening head to my grandfather's store.

Cesário Motta is now a noisy street that has been taken over by auto-mechanic workshops, cheap hairdressing salons, and dingy coffee shops. At night, transvestites and pimps frequent its broken pavement. None of this seemed to have bothered my father. After he retired, the street became his world, a world where he was well known as Doutor Alberto and where he bartered his services as a physician for free lunches, groceries, and sundry little favors. He also owned apartments in several buildings along the street, and, therefore, could not afford to live far from his doorman José, his enabler and partner in the real-estate business. The doorman was a bulky man who sweated profusely. A multitude of droplets glinted permanently on his brow, and patches of sweat stained perennially the underside of his shirtsleeves. It took a while to get accustomed to the pungent smell that emanated from his armpits. Walking past the shabby façade of my father's building, I saw José sitting in his glass cage and, reflexively, as if my father could come out of the building at any moment, I stepped up my pace. My heart pounding, I recalled the years I had guiltily avoided my father, and, feeling something akin to phantom pain, I realized that I missed him, warts and all.

As bad as mine was, Maurice's sense of loss ran far deeper than my own. It had shattered his defenses with a virulence that had incapacitated him for several years. When his mother followed his father to the other world, Maurice withdrew further into himself than would normally be expected. In a matter of weeks his grief held him incommunicado. Instead of the blueprints he had asked for, his boss at Ford Brasil began to receive esoteric reports resembling astrological charts. Compassionate as he was, the supervisor arranged for a paid leave and sent Maurice to a therapist. But Maurice only got worse. When the police found him roaming the streets in his pajamas talking nonsense to himself, his relatives had no choice but to put him in a private clinic for the mentally disturbed.

The last time I visited he was about to leave the clinic. He had almost fully recovered and was as normal as he would ever get. He was then obsessed by the nature of time. A mathematician in the clinic had given him a book on Gödel's extreme solution to Einstein's equations of general relativity. Gödel's remarkable solution, which fascinated Maurice, defined a possible universe that contained space-time paths unlike any we know, space-time paths so extreme that they made possible time loops such that one could move forward toward the future yet at the same time arrive

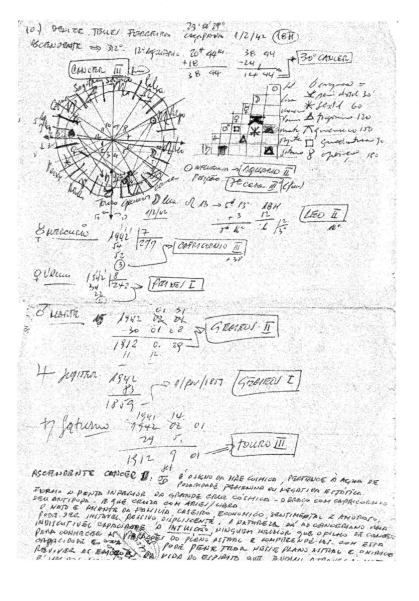

to the past. In a universe where time looped in this way, provided one traveled at a speed close to that of light, a traveler could move always forward and at one point meet his younger self. Gödel's point was a philosophical one. His intention was to show that in geometrizing time, Einstein had obliterated time as we intuitively understand it. If time travel is possible, Gödel argued, and one can return to one's past, then the past has never passed at all. Therefore, time as we intuitively understand it could not exist in Einstein's universe.

Mesmerized by Gödel's argument of the inexistence of time, Maurice had taken it to lengths at once charming and alarming. Maurice thought that if Gödel's argument, which Einstein reluctantly endorsed, had any validity and time did not really exist, it followed that no one ever aged or died. "You have always existed," Maurice told me, "in all your forms, as a baby, adolescent, young man, mature man, and the elderly man you will become. This is true of all of us. Aging, or the passage of time, is an illusion. The reason why we see only one person, you as you are now, for instance, is that we lack the focus and concentration needed to see the other, hidden, worlds around us. Should we focus enough, like mediums do, we would be able to access the people who have seemingly disappeared. You told me yourself that on occasion you see your father walking the streets. You believe you're hallucinating. But you are not. Your father is here, all the time, but it takes the kind of focus acute grief sometimes brings to see the so-called departed. I see my mother often, and sometimes we even manage a short conversation."

I must have given Maurice the impression that I was looking at an alien fallen from another planet. "I know what you are thinking," he said, somewhat defensively. "How do so many parallel worlds coexist in space? How are they sealed from one another? I mean, what is the architecture of such a universe? What, exactly, hides the babies we once were from us, and us from these baby versions of ourselves? Are there mental or actual physical veils between these worlds?

"Well," he concluded, "I confess that I don't know the answers to all these questions, but I'm working hard to find them."

Maurice asked me what I thought about all this. I did my best to reassure him that his theory was plausible, but I must say that I was alarmed by his crazy ideas about time, aging, and mortality. Maurice was denying his mother's death, which didn't augur well for his future mental health. Later, however, I reconsidered my point of view. Perhaps Maurice's belief in the inexistence of time was necessary to his living a relatively normal life. Maurice had to find a form of existence for his dead mother, and Gödel's universe offered him one. My friend's implausible beliefs might then be a sign of health rather than of disease, the raft that would keep him afloat rather than the stone that would drag him to the bottom of the sea. Time (or if it doesn't exist, whatever happened since then) has so far borne out this conjecture of mine, as Maurice had been living by himself, and successfully so.

Maurice is fortunate in other ways too. Having inherited a fair amount of money, he is free to pursue his interests in physics, zoology, botany, and literature, as well as to devote himself to his collection of dung beetles. The dazzling diversity of these beetles, which differ widely in size, shape, color, and horn, is a subject of great interest to Maurice. I learned from him that there are more than four thousand species of dung beetles, many of which come in iridescent colors of great beauty. As their name suggests, dung beetles feed on the excrement of herbivores. Adult beetles squeeze and suck the juice from the manure, while larvae feed on the undigested plant fiber in the dung, and neither adult nor larvae need eat or drink anything else. Some dung beetles live and breed in the dung heaps left by animals, while others excavate tunnels under the heap and haul the excrement down there before they feed and lay their eggs. The most interesting of the species are the so-called dung rollers, who scrape up the dung and shape it into a ball that they subsequently roll away from the heap to a suitable burial place. There the female lays her egg in the dung ball. The c-shaped larva, the grub, feeds on the fibers in the dung before pupating within a cell in the remains of the excrement. When it is ready, the new adult will dig itself out and fly to a heap of fresh dung.

Maurice thought beetles beautiful. "I cannot understand," he once told me, "why people find them repulsive. Think of Kafka's *Metamorphosis*. Kafka turned Gregor Samsa into the worst, most abject form of life he could think of: a beetle. He thought he was magnifying the horror of his tale by transforming Gregor into a 'monstrous' insect. Now why would anyone think of a three-foot beetle as monstrous? I myself would be fond of it, much like the cleaning woman in Kafka's story. She is the only one who is affectionate toward Gregor. 'Come along, you old dung beetle,' she tells him.

"In ancient Egypt, scarabs, which are dung beetles, were worshipped, and ancient Egyptians made beautiful faience scarab amulets. The sphere that appears above the head of a scarab in amulets represents both the sun and a dung ball. The Egyptians noticed how the adult beetles spring out of the dung ball and thought that they came into being by a mysterious act of self-creation. That's why the scarab beetle, *kheper*, became the god, *Khepri*, who had a man's body and a scarab's head. Egyptians believed that just as the scarab rolls the dung ball to a safe place, *Khepri*, the scarab-headed god, rolls the ball of the sun across the sky from east to west during the course of a day. During the night the god rolls the sun through the underworld back to the eastern horizon to create the next day. Each morning the god thus resurrects the sun and gives life to the world. According to the *Book of the Dead, khepher,* the scarab, could also restore life to the dead. A special kind of amulet, known as a heart scarab, was placed close to the heart of the mummy before it was wrapped. It was inscribed with a spell that allowed the deceased to transform themselves into any living creature they wished to become," Maurice said, and as he spoke, I could not help but speculate that he had found in the dung beetle yet another bizarre way of resurrecting the world he had lost. Even though Maurice may have not been fully aware of this, the scarab beetle kept him connected to Egypt and his childhood, to the paradise he could not afford to lose. The insect's association with change and rebirth must have kindled in him the hope that he would one day see his mother again.

Maurice now stood on the sidewalk in one of his old rumpled suits. It struck me as odd that a man whose body seemed too thin and frail to carry his own large head could shoulder the weighty worlds of the cosmology he had created to assuage his grief. Knowing that Maurice was averse to effusive displays of affection, I greeted him circumspectly and asked if we should walk up to Rua da Consolação, from where it would be easier to hail a taxi to the cemetery. For this was the purpose of our meeting: to visit the Jewish Cemetery of Butantã. A large, modern graveyard inaugurated only a few years before Egyptian Jews arrived in São Paulo, Butantã is now the main Jewish cemetery. Many Egyptian Jews who immigrated to the city in the late fifties are now buried there.

No sooner had Maurice and I stepped into the taxi than he put his hand in his suit pocket and produced a small box wrapped in silvery paper. "This is for you," he said.

I had promised to say a prayer, *El Malei Rachamim* (God full of compassion), over his parents' graves. The present was his way of showing his appreciation. Maurice couldn't read Hebrew and vehemently refused to read a transliteration. He claimed that such a soulless reading would be meaningless, a claim I suspect betrayed a hidden wish to communicate with his dead mother. Maurice had no doubt arrived at the conclusion that properly recited in Hebrew, like some sort of magical incantation, the prayer would take him one step closer to her. When I assented to recite the prayer, I refrained from informing him that Deuteronomy warns against directing prayers to the deceased. According to Deuteronomy, using the dead as interlocutors is an abhorrent form of pagan spirituality. Prayers at graveside must be directed only to God. In withholding this information from my friend I told myself that even though I knew Maurice's intention was blasphemous, since I would not direct the prayer to his mother, neither he nor I could be accused of blasphemy. Legally speaking this got us off the hook, but I wasn't so sure about the moral standing of my little ploy.

I unwrapped my gift and unveiled a box with a transparent lid. Inside, pinned to dark velvet, lay a giant beetle. This superb insect had a black head with two long horns, one curving upward, the other downward, and olive-green forewings sprinkled with small black spots. Maurice told me this was a very special beetle called Dynastes Hercules, a species of Scarabaeidae also known as a "rhinoceros" beetle. "It isn't a dung beetle," he said. "The Hercules beetles feed on rotting vegetables and fruit.

"They are extremely interesting," Maurice said, his owlish eyes taking over his entire face. "They are fatally attracted to light. They fly straight into campfire and return again and again to the flames, no matter how much you try to save them. During the mating season, when the rains come, males engage in duels of a most peculiar kind. They face off and make threatening head-bobbing movements that produce a shrill chirping sound. Things can get nasty. One beetle will cut the other to pieces with his horns. The victorious beetle will show off by dragging the mangled corpse of his opponent before the other beetles, like Achilles did with Hector." After explaining how this show was put on to impress the females of the species, Maurice went on to give a detailed explanation of how sexual attraction occurs among beetles. He lectured on the minutiae of sex pheromones, the chemicals females emit to attract the male scarabs, and he kept on lecturing until the taxi deposited us at the cemetery's entrance.

There are about thirty thousand graves at the Jewish cemetery of Butantã. Rectangular slabs of stone laid flat on the ground, the graves are arranged in terraces down the slopes of a hill. The rows of graves are separated by narrow paths that can be reached through the avenues that loop around the various sections of the grounds. Maurice's gait stiffened as we walked up the hill toward his parents' graves. He did not say a word. When we reached his mother's grave, he took a folded sheet of paper out of his interior breast pocket and, handing it to me, asked me to read the prayer. I knew the prayer by heart, but not wanting in any way to disrupt my friend's concentration, I unfolded the sheet on which he had painstakingly copied the Hebrew words. I read slowly and carefully, pausing more often than necessary for fear of making a mistake that might cut off Maurice's secret communication with the beyond. After I had finished the prayers, Maurice lingered by his mother's tomb while I walked up to where my grandparents and father were buried. By a strange coincidence they lay between Alameda Gad and Alameda Acher, my grandfather's name and surname.

I stood by my grandparents' gray marble graves and conjured them up in my mind. I shut my eyes and saw them in their apartment at Rua Fortunato bickering, as old couples often do, over some trivial matter. She had displaced his glasses somewhere, and he couldn't find them. He was in his striped flannel pajamas looking for his glasses on every surface of the living room, while she sat in her blue nightgown watching the news. When I beheld them clearly in my imagination I recited the prayer, first for my grandmother, than for him. A wind of grief blew through me as I laid pebbles on their tombstones.

Feeling the usual dread I experience when I try to picture him, I then walked toward my father's grave. When it comes to my father, I often dredge up a face that resembles the fanged physiognomy of a wrathful deity from Tibet. Luckily, on that clear day, my father appeared in a good mood. A young cypress watched over us as I recited the *Malei*. Maurice stood stiffly beside me, as uneasy as he and I once were when we sat beside our fathers on the synagogue's bench.

The Sephardic temple we attended in São Paulo was, by a curious, though inappropriate coincidence, located at Rua da Abolição, a street celebrating the abolition of slavery. The synagogue became known as the Temple of Abolition, a name that fits the first Exodus, though not the second. Many of the Jews who left Egypt in 1956 were wealthy, not slaves, and rather than coming out of bondage, they felt expelled from paradise. As the Sephardic community grew, the different groups split and formed their own synagogues. Egyptian Jews took eight years to build their own luxurious temple. In the meantime, the congregation attended service in an old house on a quiet street called Rua Brigadeiro Galvão. In this provisional synagogue, Maurice and I sat silently next to our fathers. We could not understand a single word of the prayers, and although on occasion moved by the mysterious rituals and incantations, we were for the most part bored beyond endurance. Together we attended Hebrew school, run by a large-bellied man with a forbidding beard who wielded the ruler freely. He took great pleasure in rapping our knuckles whenever we made a mistake. The memory of that fat man swatting his wide-eyed, stringy pupils nearly threw me into laughter.

I saw Maurice again on Saturday, my last day in São Paulo. We walked down Cesário Motta in the direction of Largo do Arouche. The faces of the men drinking at a bar's doorstep shone in the sun, and the smell of sweat, alcohol, and tobacco followed us for a block. At the corner Maurice and I said our good-byes, and, thankful for the chance to see him, I watched him go, his large head balanced precariously on his slender neck. I then walked to the flower stand across the street from the shoe store that once was my grandfather's shop.

Named after my sister, *Marie France Tecidos Finos* was a miniature replica of my grandfather's store in Cairo. I sat on a green bench, beside pots of begonias the color of sunset, and gazed at the shoe store. The shoes gradually faded, and I saw instead the fabrics in the window of my grandfather's shop. I saw the red and blue letters of my sister's name above the old shop's front window, the same window behind which Reinaldo, the youngest of two clerks, and I would wrap the mannequins' lean bodies in luxurious fabrics. We favored the golden brocades and shiny silks, but my grandfather insisted that simpler fabrics also were creatures of God. A debate usually followed. Negotiations weren't always amicable, yet our angry exchanges had a way of turning into bursts of laughter. And when it was all done we would sit down to feast on the chocolate éclairs my grandfather bought for such occasions.

My grandfather liked to watch people's faces when they savored sweets. He received his clients with an old-fashioned Middle Eastern hospitality, offering them coffee and pastries. A virtuoso salesman, he could entrance three or four clients at a time. He would hold a piece of fabric against a woman's cheek and marvel at the effect, as if the fabric were a magic wand that turned any woman into a beauty. Reinaldo and I would watch astounded as the women left the store loaded with merchandise they had never intended to buy. Gently coaching the good-looking Reinaldo, my grandfather patiently explained that he had to listen to a client as if she were saying the most fascinating thing in the world. "Pretend they are telling you," he would say, "that you won a fortune in the lottery, and imagine all the things you are going to buy with the money."

"Most of all," he'd caution, "don't try to seduce them. Don't be obvious. Just listen, listen, listen. That's the greatest aphrodisiac. Don't worry about selling; just make them feel good about themselves." Reinaldo was young, and he inevitably made mistakes that enervated my grandfather, but though skirmishes sometimes ensued, the two men liked each other too much to hold a grudge. Reinaldo's devotion was touching. When my grandfather wasn't feeling well, Reinaldo doted on him with a sad puppy's expression on his face.

I spent many an afternoon sitting by the blonde-wood counter with both of them, and it was there that I learned in bits and pieces why my grandfather Gad had left Smyrna for Cairo. He had left in 1910, when he was sixteen. At the time thirty thousand Jews, about a seventh of the total population, lived in the Jewish quarter of Smyrna. My grandfather's family, all eight of them, lived in a small wooden house: his father, David Acher; his mother, Rebecca, born Hadjes; and the six brothers, Leon, Moise, Simon, Gad, Macabee, and Dan. Like most Ottoman cities of the time, Smyrna was divided into ethnic-religious quarters. The Turkish quarter lay at the southern end of the city against the slopes of Mount Pagus. Just below it was the Jewish quarter, and farther to the north, the Armenian and Greek neighborhoods. The French quarter bordered the water. There you could find movie houses, theatres, embassies, sidewalk cafés, and boutiques packed with the latest fashions from Paris. Travel reports and diaries from the turn of the century invariably tell of the striking contrast between the European city fronting the sea and the Turkish one skirting the slopes of Mount Pagus—a contrast that drew out the mix of nostalgia and resentment my grandfather harbored for his native city.

"If you entered the Gulf of Smyrna," he once said, "and saw the city from a distance, Smyrna would appear as a glittering Sheherazadian dream; but if you docked and went inside, in the poorer quarters, you would see a very different picture. The French quarter was nice, but the Turkish and Jewish quarters were not. We lived in narrow streets and little wooden houses that had room for only half of the people who lived in them. My family was lucky. Most families lived ten or twelve people to a room in hovels that stank. Some streets smelled of excrement and sour milk; it was terrible. We weren't the poorest because my father, God bless him, had a tiny fabric store, a hole in the wall. I learned everything I know from him, and I enjoyed every minute we spent together. He was a pious man, but he was also great fun. We had a decent life thanks to him, and the street where we lived wasn't so bad. We were poor, but we didn't live like many Jews did in those filthy houses, sleeping on the ground, a family of ten or more eating rotten food from the same plate. I suppose that to Frenchmen like Pierre Loti it was very exciting to dress up in a fez and baggy pants and smoke hashish, but young men wanted to get out of there fast. We wanted to go to the fabulous Paris of our dreams. We were in love with France and Paris. We went to school at the Alliance Française Universelle, where we learned French and almost forgot the archaic Spanish we spoke at home. The Spanish we spoke was almost the same as the Spanish that Jews spoke in fifteenth century Andalusia. Our ancestors brought it to Turkey when they ran from the Inquisition.

"It wasn't easy to leave Smyrna. I loved my parents, and I had a lot of friends there, and I can't say I didn't enjoy my life in the city. But after the Young Turks came to power, staying in Turkey was no longer an option for my brothers and me. The Young Turks wanted to restore the constitutional monarchy, and they forced Sultan Abdul Hamid II to recall parliament in 1908. In the end they kicked the sultan out anyway. Many Jews supported the Young Turks and the unionist government. My father and teachers at the Alliance Française liked them, and the Jewish newspaper *La Boz del Pueblo* praised the Young Turks to the skies. The problems began when the new government threatened to enforce compulsory military service. In the Ottoman Empire this meant you would go to war for sure, and your chances of coming back in one piece were zero. My older brothers Leon and Moise left Smyrna first, Leon to Cairo and Moise to Buenos Aires. Two years later, after Leon had found a steady job at Cicurel, the rest of the brothers followed. I was almost seventeen, and I worked at Cicurel for fifteen years, until I opened my own store with Leon.

"We opened it close to Cicurel, on a side street off Rue Fouad, a wide boulevard where you could find all the fancy shops. I was thirty-two years old, and I felt like a king. I had my own store, and it was doing well; I was getting rich. I was happily married and head over heels in love with your grandmother. She was gorgeous with her dark hair and large blue eyes. Her parents also were from Turkey, from Istanbul, and they spoke Spanish and Ladino like we did, and I liked them. Everything was going very well for me. The only sadness, the only regret I had, was leaving my father and mother behind. They wouldn't leave, not even when the Greeks seized Smyrna in 1919, nor when the Turks took the city back in 1922. My parents disappeared in 1922, but I don't think Turkish soldiers killed them. Soldiers had received orders to protect the Jews, because Jews had always sided with the Turks. I was told that Turkish officers asked Jews to mark their houses so they could be spared the rage of their soldiers. The officers must have read the Bible.

"It was a blessing that the Turks took Smyrna back. That's what saved the Jews of Smyrna from the Nazis. The Salonica Jews weren't so lucky. The Turks never took Salonica back from the Greeks. Turkey was neutral in World War II, but the Greeks were not. So only Salonica was occupied and all its Jews rounded up and sent to concentration camps. But this doesn't mean that the Turks are angels.

"In 1922 the troops of Mustafa Kemal entered Smyrna and massacred the Greeks and the Armenians. The soldiers burned down the Greek and Armenian quarters and killed everyone in their path: men, women, and children. The Turks claim it was the Greeks and Armenians who burned the city, but I don't believe it. You remember Menachem? My friend who comes here to chat once in a while? Well, he was there. To this day, it causes him pain to talk about what he saw. From the window of his house, Menachem and his family saw Turkish soldiers rape their neighbor's wife in front of her husband and little girl, and then slaughter them with their bayonets. There were corpses strewn along the streets and floating in the water. The sea was red. Menachem told me that all night long they heard screams and gunshots and people begging for their lives. While the city burned, thousands took whatever belongings they could and ran to the docks. They knocked each other down to get on whatever boat was available. But there weren't enough boats. Allied warships anchored in the bay, in shouting distance of the massacre, did absolutely nothing.

"My poor parents," my grandfather moaned. "My poor parents," he almost howled. "I wish I had dragged them out of Smyrna by force. They disappeared during the Turkish recapture. Probably burned. Sometimes my whole body hurts when I think of them. My mother was a dark beauty, a true Spaniard. Odette looked just like her. Your mother's nickname was L'Espagnole.

"Your mother," my grandfather began—but he could not (he never could) say anything more. His eyes teared, and he choked, and I, wanting to spare him or myself or both of us, quickly pointed my finger in Reinaldo's direction, indicating that the young clerk clumsily unfolding fabric for a client needed my grandfather's immediate help.

My grandfather never, not once, said that his daughter had died. The closest he ever got to admitting she was dead was on the eve of our departure from Cairo. He told my sister and me that he and my grandmother were staying behind for a short while because he needed to sell his shop and put his affairs in order. But it was obvious that this would take far longer than a "short while." My grandfather sat us on the sofa and kneeled before us. "Don't you worry," he said. "Your grandmother and I will never leave you. We promised your mother we would always take care of you, and we always will." Then he broke down and cried, and my sister, who was six at the time, also began to cry. I watched as my grandfather put his hands over his eyes, and I wished I could make him stop. He was the only person with whom I felt carefree, light, and almost joyful. The happiest days of my life as a child were spent in his company. I remember playing with him at the beach at Ras el Bar or at his store, where he would greet me with open arms, or at home, at bedtime, when he told me the stories of Sinbad and Ali Baba. It surprised me when he cried. Although at times I had caught glimpses of his despair, it had not occurred to me that he was an unhappy man. He was careful not to show me his somber side, bearing his pain with a smile on his face—and happy is how I wanted him to be. I did not want to see him sob like a baby; I did not want to feel helpless; I did not want to feel the sense of futility that was furtively making itself known to me; and, most of all, I did not want to miss him as much as I missed him even before I left Cairo. But he would not stop crying, and I could not make him stop. I didn't have the requisite skills yet. It would take time to learn a few tricks, to learn how to distract him, to help him forget—to offer him brief moments of reprieve.

IV

Al-Bassatin, Cairo

Floating in a murky chaos, I heard sounds of splashing water and laughter. Then darkness cleared, and I stood among children playing at the shallow edge of a swimming pool. Belly down on a pink air mattress, a girl paddled and giggled as her mother helped her along. Two boys jostled each other in a confusion of foam, and, closer to my father and me, a boy pinched his nose and exploded into the pool. I watched, anxious, as my father knelt on the turquoise tiles and showed me how to breathe. "Keep your head down. Keep it down," he ordered.

Nothing about the pool or the people in it allowed me to identify its location. It could have been in Cairo, either at the Tawfekieh Club or the Gezira Sporting Club, or in São Paulo, at the Hebraica. My father and I spent much of our time together in one swimming pool or another. He worshipped the sun and loved to swim, and one of his lifelong projects was to make a great swimmer out of me. I was thrilled by my father's attention, yet felt inadequate to the task. My thin and freckled arms refused to master the water as his powerful bronzed ones did. Whenever I swam to the far end of the pool, my heart crumbled as I imagined the headshake of disapproval with which he would greet me when I returned. I hoped my promises of improvement would keep his interest in me, if not keen, at least alive, but I lived in dread of a final rejection. In the swimming pool I felt at once the exhilaration of being the focus of my father's attention and the disappointment of falling short of his approval. To this day my affection for glinting turquoise water comes mingled with a piercing malaise, a composite feeling of failure and unrequited love.

Water dripping from his brown torso, my father ordered me to swim the dooming laps. My heart raced as I readied myself. I plunged in, but just as I began to lift my arm out of the water, the cries and splashing sounds grew wild and deafening. I then woke, sweaty and confused, finding myself in a dark room I did not immediately recognize. Only after my eyes adjusted to the dimness, and the television set emerged solid and black from the shadows, did I remember I was in Cairo. I had booked a room at the Marriott in Zamalek, a short walk away from the apartment where I had lived as a child. The squeals and splashing sounds I had heard in my dream now came from the hotel's pool.

I pulled open the curtains and stepped into the blinding light of the balcony. Down below, a topiary garden separated the pool area from the blue umbrellas shading the tables of an open-air café. The marine umbrellas brought to mind a childhood memory of a parasol that put me on an unnamed yet familiar beach, breathing in the salty air and delighting in sights of azure water and frothy waves, and I would have stayed there for a long time had it not been for a sudden pang of apprehension alerting me that on the previous evening I had invited Magdi Fanous to lunch. A former student of mine, he was the only person I knew in Cairo, and though I had not intended to call him, an unforeseen fear of being alone in the city had driven me to dial his number.

My plane had landed late in the afternoon of the previous day, and a taxi had driven me to the Marriott just before sunset. Through the windows of the cab I watched Cairo dissolve into a mist as nebulous as my memories of her, and with the dying day came a queasiness that nibbled at my insides and tempted me to order the driver back to the airport.

At the hotel I was taken to a room that had the usual wall-to-wall carpet and the usual two beds separated by the usual bedside table. The headboards and table were stained a red finish and so was the dresser on which stood the television set. I lay down on the bed and pressed the remote control's power button. The television made a popping sound, and President Mubarak appeared in his customary dark suit reviewing the troops in the Suez town of Ismailia. I had forgotten that on October 6, the day I arrived, Egyptians celebrate a victory against Israel. On that day, in 1973, the Egyptian army had broken through the Bar Lev line and almost won the war.

I watched Mubarak salute the troops with a growing sense of estrangement. To my chagrin, I felt like a tourist. I was no revenant, no pilgrim. Just an aging man with a burning desire to remember what he could not; a foolish man wanting to believe that memory was a matter of geography. It was the distress this realization caused me that drove me to call Magdi. Adrift in this foreign city I needed the anchoring reassurance I hoped he could provide. The warmth with which he greeted me on the phone and his willingness to meet me for lunch the following day had the comforting effect I had hoped for—and now, baking on my balcony, my heart raced as I checked my watch and saw that I had almost missed our appointment.

When he saw me, Magdi scurried from under the umbrella and grabbed my hand. A bear of a man, bald and tanned, he wore old-fashioned, thick-framed glasses. His gaze was at once stern and forgiving, the gaze of a man who, though not particularly pious, had nevertheless the makings of a saint. Magdi was a Copt who had devoted himself to improving the lives of the thirty thousand Coptic garbage collectors, the *zabbaleen*, who live in the slums of the Mokattam hills. He had been working for years to provide the garbage collectors' settlement with piped water, electricity, sewerage, a school, and a health center.

Formerly pig breeders from southern Egypt, these Coptic villagers had fallen on bad times and moved to Cairo, where they make a living by recycling the waste they collect. They feed the organic waste to the pigs they sell to hotels, restaurants, and non-Muslim residents, melt oil containers they sell to plastic manufacturers, and recycle used bags, clothes, hangers, pitchers, tin, glass, and animal bones. Although they created an efficient system of waste disposal, because they process the refuse within their own living quarters, the Coptic garbage collectors live in horrid conditions. The foul-smelling, disease-ridden Mokattam lanes are heaped with mounds of paper, manure, tin cans, and animal carcasses, which are periodically burned into clouds of smoke that hang black over the city. Women and children work amid the garbage and rotting food used to feed their pigs and goats, and they often get hurt when they sort through broken glass, rusted metal, and other dangerous materials collected from hospitals.

Magdi's bold pate glistened in the sun as he shook my hand. His grin was infectious. We sat down, and Magdi said he missed our long conversations on painting. Years ago he had written a thesis on the politics of public health in Egypt, an astute essay on the various schemes by which public health funds were misappropriated for private and political ends. But Magdi's true passion lay elsewhere. He loved art and art history, especially surrealism and Dada. At one point he had planned to write a book about Marcel Duchamp, whose visual puns and mockery of the art world had fascinated him for years. I never understood why, for Magdi did not seem to be drawn to the absurd. On the contrary, he had a strong sense of mission that betrayed a belief in a meaningful and ultimately benevolent universe. I can only speculate that Duchamp's iconoclastic humor afforded Magdi an escape from his cramped moral self.

Magdi's voice boomed inside the shade of the umbrella. "You finally returned," he said. "I hope this city of ours won't get to you as badly as it gets to me. Cairo still has its attractions, but she is now like a fading Hollywood star: you can barely see the beauty in the wrinkles of her withered face. Zamalek is nothing like the lush island it was when you left. Maybe I'm exaggerating, but aside from the green patch of the Gezira Sporting Club and some of the streets close to this hotel, even Zamalek is deteriorating. Some parts of the island have become almost slummy. You must remember the quiet streets with the bright red flamboyant trees in bloom. Well, most of them are gone. And the old European city downtown is also in bad shape. The old buildings are still standing around Soliman Pasha, but they are dirty, run down, plastered with cheap advertising placards and graffiti. The entire city is now buried under elevated avenues and overpasses, and jammed with automobiles.

Magdi stopped talking and stared at me as if he were surprised by my presence. "I'm sorry," he finally said. "I did not mean to discourage you right at the start of your visit. I don't know what you are expecting to find, and I suppose I felt the need to protect you from disappointment. I'm accustomed to receiving people from all over the world who come here thinking of exotic spice and jasmine, and I feel I have to instruct them in the realities on the ground, to give them an idea of what it is like to live in the slums of Chubra and Mokattam."

I assured Magdi I had not come to Cairo chasing after the fragrance of jasmine. I told him I had no illusion of finding the city of my boyhood, a city that in any case I hardly remembered. Yet, even as I spoke, I knew this was not entirely true. I *was* chasing after a dream. Uncle Victor's old friends had lamented the city's decay in more or less the same words Magdi had used. They had revisited the places memory had sacralized—their old house, school, temple, and the streets they once loved—only to be disappointed by their state of disrepair. To these disconsolate pilgrims their once golden city, real or imagined, had forever vanished. As sympathetic as I was, I could not identify with their plight. My affliction was different. My recollections never amounting to more than a vapor, I envied the older pilgrims their vivid memories. Whereas they rejected wholesale the city's present, I embraced it, hoping it would bring back the past I had forgotten. I wanted to remember the boy I once was, the boy who held his mother's hand in the old photographs. I wished the city would allow me to authenticate the pictures, to confirm the boy's identity as my own.

"You've just arrived," Magdi said, "and here I am discouraging you with all this dark talk about Cairo. I've been in a bad mood lately because things aren't going well at Mokattam. For a while we succeeded in cleaning up the settlement. The Ford Foundation gave the garbage collectors more money to truck their garbage to a nearby dump, and everything went well until the owners of the trucks paid all their installments. Then they began to slack off. They had no incentive, you see, to continue collecting garbage from the households. The trucks could no longer be taken away from them, so they started throwing waste in the streets again. You tell them over and over again that it is not good for their children, but no matter how much you say it, they don't stop throwing the garbage in the streets unless you force them, or give them monetary rewards. On top of everything, the government closed the nearby municipal dump, forcing them to drive fifty kilometers away from the settlement to dump their garbage.

"It's an uphill battle," Magdi sighed, his mouth sagging at the corners. "It really breaks my heart to see the kids playing in that filth." Magdi threw his hands up. "What more can I do?" he groaned.

His forlorn glance made me want to distract him, to draw his attention away from his worries. I told him he was doing more than most people do, and, changing subjects, asked him if he had finished the book he was writing on Duchamp. "Since I last saw you," he said, "I lost interest in Duchamp. I fell in love with Max Ernst after I saw an exhibition of his early work. A series of collages with gouache drew my attention, especially one in which Ernst had assembled a lung, a heart, intestines, and other parts of animal anatomy. The painting made me think of the science fiction experiments where mismatched parts of humans and animals are stitched together to create laboratory monsters. It reminded me of war, of the mutilations inflicted on soldiers. I don't know if you've ever seen this little painting. It has a weird title; something like *Stratified Rock with Lava*, followed by two other incomprehensible lines. The painting made a powerful impression on me because at the time I was working at the health center in Mokattam. I was seeing a lot of people with horrid wounds. I never thought of the insides of the human body as anything but repulsive, yet Ernst succeeded in turning his assembled organs into something beautiful.

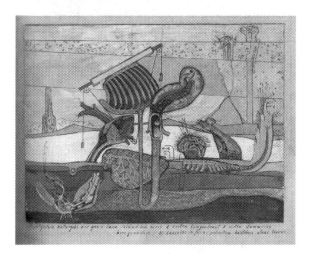

"This may be crazy," Magdi continued, "but as I looked at the painting from a distance, I saw a boat. Ernst had placed a rib cage on a mast of sorts, and I saw it as the sail of a ship gliding among sea anemones. I was reminded of the ancient Egyptian ships described in the *Book of the Dead*, the ships that carried the dead on their final journey through the underworld. After seeing *Stratified Rock* I became obsessed with Ernst's gouaches. Have you seen these? They are a kind of negative, or inverse collage, if you will, because Ernst conceals some objects with paint while integrating the others into dreamlike images. Ernst's images seduce you with their beauty and then challenge you to find the secret connections between the seemingly unrelated objects they depict. His montages are absurd, impossible, yet, at least for me, they seem oddly familiar and make sense. It is as if I had seen them before, in my dreams perhaps, and had grasped their meaning.

"One of his photomontages has stayed with me ever since I saw it, years ago. It shows an X-rayed fish flying over a ship made with the internal organs of an inverted beetle. It is extraordinary.

"Ernst called it *Here Everything is Still Floating*," Magdi continued—but he could not finish his thought. A waiter had finally noticed us and come to take our orders. We ordered *taamiya*

sandwiches and beer, and Magdi continued to talk about his esthetic adventures in Max Ernst's world. His enthusiasm pleased me, as I was happy to see him momentarily freed from his worries. When we finished eating our sandwiches, Magdi said he had to leave. He hesitated for a moment and then asked me if I needed help getting around the city. "I know," he said, "how personal this trip is to you, and I imagine you may want to visit some places alone. So I will not insist. I will leave it up to you. You have my phone numbers. If you need me for anything, please call me."

Energized by Magdi's visit, I decided to walk to the building where I had lived for the first nine years of my life. Uncle Victor had told me the building was on Gezira Street, a few blocks from the Marriott. He had described it as being ten stories high, the color of sand, with long balconies that rounded the corners on all four sides. The building was next to a beautiful villa, once owned by Mahmoud Khalil, a famous politician who had amassed an impressive collection of paintings. At the reception desk I asked a young moustachioed man for a map and directions, and he, with a dramatic flourish of the hand, opened the map and drew a circle around a small block near the hotel. "This is the Mahmoud Khalil villa," he said, "but it isn't a museum anymore." With yet another flourish of the hand, he drew a second circle on the map. "The museum moved here," he said, writing the address on the margin. After insisting I wished to visit the villa, he said I could easily reach it by walking through the parking lot at the back of the hotel.

I followed his instructions and walked among the sharp-edged shadows cast by the hot afternoon sun. In a few minutes I stood facing the neo-Islamic villa of Mahmoud Khalil. With its shuttered windows and locked doors, the white villa sat on a well-tended lawn as majestic and purposeless as a regally dressed princess in an empty ballroom.

Across the street was the wall of the Gezira Sporting Club, a wall I did not remember, and a block ahead I could see the balconies ribbing the sand-colored building I was looking for. I cannot be sure whether it was the building itself I recognized or my uncle's description of it, or perhaps a picture someone may have shown me years ago. My family lived on the sixth floor, facing Giza, and I think it was from there we saw the bombing of Cairo during the Suez War. We would hear the hum of the planes, then the muffled explosions, and a second later the sky would light up. But on that night, the night my grandfather had said his tearful good-byes, no bombs could be heard. The British and French had withdrawn, and we had to leave Egypt. The balcony's shutters where closed, and the lights were on in the living room when my grandfather wept before my sister and me. Of this room I remember only the velvet sofa on which I sat and the Bokhara rug on which he kneeled. As I approached the building's entrance, the red carpet and my grandfather's face loomed large in my mind. His eyes were pleading, as if he were asking for my forgiveness. Had he seen anger in my eyes? Had I felt he, like my mother, was letting me down? Had his eyes been as lovingly guilty as I now remembered them?

A tall, swarthy man in robe and turban stood guarding the lobby. In the dimness behind him a winding staircase hugged the iron cage of a sinister elevator. Many of my worst dreams feature cagelike elevators, but these nightmares could be the result of the film noirs I have seen. Had I really climbed those stairs? Had I taken that elevator? If I had, I could not remember. I approached the forbidding figure at the entrance and, after discovering he spoke some French, explained that I would like to revisit the apartment where I had lived as a child. He smiled in sympathy but shook his head. "*Vacances*," he said. The current tenants were on vacation for the next two weeks; without their permission he could not let me in. Bribing people doesn't come easily to me, so it was with some embarrassment that I put my hand in my pocket. But the doorman guessed my intent, shook his head again, and said, "*Non, Monsieur.*" I thanked him, and mortified as I was, walked away as fast as I could. Around the corner I took snapshots of the sixth-floor balcony and then walked aimlessly along the streets of Zamalek until I found my way to the end of Asis Ozman Street.

There I studied the old villa that once housed the Gezira Preparatory School, but nothing, neither the whole nor the parts, looked remotely familiar. Of that street I have only memories of my father waiting outside the school. A cigarette in the corner of his mouth, he would be leaning against his yellow Ford convertible. I always thought of the Ford as an airplane because its shiny chrome grille looked like an old propeller. When he saw me coming, my father would flick away his cigarette, lift me into the car, and we would drive into the wind singing old French songs like "Alouette, Gentille Allouette."

I could see my father leaning against the yellow Ford, but I could not recognize the villa. Looking at it I had the same sense of estrangement I felt when I first saw the only picture I have of my class at the preparatory school. In the picture, six of us are sitting at a table facing the camera. Behind us a teacher stands in front of a blackboard on which the date, 20 February 1953, is written in white chalk. The boy in the left corner I have learned to identify as myself is five years and seven months old. He has lost his mother two months ago. She disappeared suddenly, and the boy was told she went away on a long trip. Does he believe he's been told the truth? He must sense something is wrong, because he must have seen her sick in her bed. But can he really understand she will never come back to him? I don't know the answers to these questions. The freckled boy in the corner keeps his silence. The other children in the picture smile at the photographer, but he sits ill at ease, his fingers clutching his pencil. Is he thinking of his mother? Is he frightened? Or is he just numb?

That night the boy revisited me in my hotel bed, in a dream I had not dreamt in years. The boy stood in the darkness of a long corridor at the end of which was a wedge of light from an open door. Muffled voices and moans slipped out of the room. The boy's father and other men surrounded his mother's bed, and though he could not see her, he heard her moans. A sharp cry flew like shrapnel through the darkness—and I bolted upright in my hotel bed, my heart pounding in my chest. The shadows in the room gradually lost their threat, but I could no longer sleep. My body was a house haunted by the freckled boy. What had he witnessed? How long was she sick at home before they took her away? Was she taken in an ambulance? Was the boy at home or did he stay with relatives? Mystifying as this was, I had not ever given much thought to the details surrounding my mother's illness and death.

In the morning I took a cab to Midan Talaat Harb in downtown Cairo. Formerly called Soliman Pasha, the round-point was at the heart of Ismailieh, then the fashionable European quarter of the city. A strip of land between the Nile and Islamic Cairo, Ismailieh had been a swampy plain before Khedive Ismail built a version of Hausmann's Paris on the marshy site. In the 1850s the khedive hired an army of European architects that erected a city of wide boulevards and round-points, among which were Soliman Pasha Avenue and its famous circle. This was Uncle Victor's favorite boulevard. *"La Rue Soliman Pasha,"* he once told me, *"était de toute beauté."*

We were sitting under an orange parasol, facing the spacious lawn of his house on Long Island. Aunt Isabelle poured orange juice into our glasses while Uncle Victor examined a map of Cairo through a thick magnifying glass. "Here it is," he said, putting

the tip of his finger on Talaat Harb Circle. "In my time the circle was called Soliman Pasha. The avenue that runs through it was also called Soliman Pasha. I walked on that street every single day because my clinic was just a few blocks from the circle, at number 34. Your father used to have his on Bustan Street, but then he moved next door to me, to number 37. These were beautiful buildings, you know, with apartments that had fifteen-foot ceilings and splendid friezes.

"My favorite patisserie was on the circle. It was named Groppi, after its Swiss owner, and it was located in a building facing the statue of Soliman Pasha. A marvelous art deco mosaic with golden waves and seashells against a blue background decorated the entrance to Groppi. Everybody who was anybody wanted to be seen under Groppi's glass dome. Even the royal family catered exclusively with Groppi. The Swiss made delicious ice creams with wonderful names. My favorites were "Josephine Baker," a silky chocolate sundae, and the "Marquise aux Marrons," a French vanilla ice cream studded with chunks of *marrons glacés*." Uncle Victor's hand drew an ascending spiral in the air. "They were unbelievably good," he said.

"Your mother loved the "Marquise." Isabelle and I liked to go out with her. She was full of life, always making fun of things. But she had one big problem. Odette liked to fix herself up; she spent hours in front of the mirror. Ooh la la," Uncle Victor chuckled, "it took forever.

"On weekends we sometimes took afternoon tea on the terrace of the Shepheard's Hotel and then went to Groppi's for a whiskey or a "Marquise." At the Shepheard's the likes of Farouk and Churchill sipped gin slings while the waiters glided from table to table in their red tarbooshes. Inside the hotel there was a spectacular Moorish hall. It was lit by a huge dome of colored glass and supported by tall lotus columns like those at Karnack. It was spectacular. During the war British officers swarmed the hotel and carried on as if nothing serious were happening, as if they were tourists enjoying an afternoon drink. The Shepheard's faced the beautiful Esbekiyya Gardens."

Uncle Victor pointed at a green spot on the map. Tufts of
fine black hair lined the spaces between his knuckles. "I read
somewhere," he said, "that under the Ottomans Esbekiyya was
a fancy residential area around a lake covered with water lilies.
The wealthy families who lived there took boat rides at night,
and the glowing lanterns that hung from their boats were a sight
to behold. Apparently it was Napoleon himself who had the
lake filled. He turned it into an ugly patch of dirt. Nothing was
done to embellish it until Ismail brought a landscape gardener
from Europe to create the gardens that made Esbekiyya the most
elegant place in town. But today nothing is left of the old gardens.
The Shepheard's was burned down during Black Saturday, in
1952, and now a wide avenue cuts through what remains of the
park. The avenue is an extension of the famous Fouad Street, and
it is now named 26 of July to celebrate the day King Farouk left
Egypt. Esbekiyya must be a hellhole of traffic jams and dust. But

you must go to the old Fouad Street. The elegant boutiques and major department stores like Cicurel and Oreco used to be there. Your grandfather's store was on a side street close to Cicurel. I don't remember which street it was on. Maybe you'll remember the place if you walk around the area.

"If you want to visit downtown Cairo, start at Soliman Pasha, at Groppi's, and walk up to the buildings where we had our clinics, then turn right on Adly Street and go to the pharaonic Synagogue, where your father and mother were married. I used to go there every Shabbat until the grand rabbi refused to marry Isabelle and me because she wasn't Jewish. He excommunicated me! I never set foot in the Adly synagogue after that and will never do so again. The Cairo I knew is gone. Finished. So what's the point? Anyhow, Carmen Weinstein's stationery store is on Cherif Street, not too far from the synagogue. She and her mother run the Jewish community, and they'll make the arrangements for your visit to Bassatine."

Uncle Victor stared at something at the end of his garden, or so it seemed, but it did not take me long to realize he was staring into space. His was an inward gaze, a peek at some scene in the distant past. "It's funny," he finally said. "When I was speaking to you an image flashed through my mind, something I witnessed on Black Saturday. I was paying a visit to Roger Lagnado, a friend and patient who lived in a building close to Soliman Pasha Circle, when we heard a loud bang. We rushed to the balcony to see what was happening. Down below people were cheering a man hammering away at Groppi's metal grille. When he finally brought it down the crowd stormed the café and dragged out chairs, tables, lamps, cakes, and bags of flour and sugar. They made a huge pile and set everything on fire, and then someone threw Molotov cocktails through the windows. We heard a few explosions, and flames came out of Groppi. Two men stumbled out screaming for help, but the crowd pushed them back into the fire. It was horrible to watch. Horrible. Thank God the firemen and police came and dispersed the crowd. Groppi was saved, but I have no idea what became of the poor devils who were thrown into the flames. I remember seeing dark plumes of smoke all around us, and by sunset it seemed like the crowds had burned down the whole city. The air stank. We had to close the windows and put up with the stifling heat indoors. We all knew this was coming, but we kept hoping for the best. We clung to the past, to the wonderful life we had in Cairo."

Uncle Victor shivered and fell silent. The garden had turned a shade darker under the bulbous clouds that packed the sky. Aunt Isabelle ordered us inside. Rising slowly from his chair, my uncle put his arm in mine, and we walked haltingly to the living room. With its old glass cabinets and Persian rugs, the room must have been a reproduction of Uncle Victor's Cairene salon. "Look at this," he said. "It's like a museum. I brought these carpets and knickknacks from Cairo with me. I once thought I'd leave all this stuff to my kids. But they're not really interested. The link between generations is broken. My children, your cousins, will never know what it is to be an Egyptian Jew. You were older when you left Cairo, but not even you, for all your interest in the past, know what it was really like. My generation, at most yours, is the last link, and when we are gone, Egyptian Jews will be forgotten. It will be as if we never existed."

Standing on Soliman Pasha facing Groppi, I remembered Uncle Victor's words. He was now *gone*, as he would say, and though I missed him, I was glad he had been spared the disappointment of visiting his favorite café. Groppi's marine mosaics still adorned its façade, but the interior had lost its charm. Flies buzzed over the pink cloths that covered the tables, and the cakes behind the glass counter looked old and stale. Back outside I walked around the circle and found that, despite the lamentations I had heard about their calamitous state, most buildings had not changed much since the fifties. Not that I remembered any of them. My judgment was solely based on the photographs of Soliman Pasha Circle I had studied. Six of the seven buildings that front the circle, including the neo-Baroque one that houses Groppi, were built before 1930. Only the art deco one, which once bore the winged Air France seahorse on its façade, was built around 1940.

The seven buildings, except for a few minor changes, are the same my uncle knew, and the same I must have known.

My disappointment grew with every building I examined. Everything felt familiar, yet at the same time I could not remember a single detail of the urban landscape before me. A stranger and yet not, a revenant and yet not, I could not mourn the past in a proper way. I remembered enough to feel a sense of loss but not enough to know and grieve what I had lost. I could not even lament the statue of Soliman Pasha, who, dashing in his Zouave uniform, had been replaced by that of Talaat Harb in his banker's suit. How could I complain if I did not remember the statue? Craving some memory, I found myself pasting in my mind the image of Soliman Pasha over the statue of Talaat Harb. My mental collage stuck only for a moment, after which Soliman's baggy pantaloons and curved scabbard faded back into the banker's plain trousers. Unwilling to accept defeat, I renewed my concentration and again conjured up the Zouave, only to see him turn once more into the banker. I did this a few more times, and then left the circle and walked up Soliman Pasha Avenue. The throng of people on the sidewalk, the garish windows bathed in neon light, and the honking cars gradually acquired a vividness that overwhelmed my senses. A voice within me echoed the rant against the decaying city I had often heard at Uncle Victor's home on Long Island. A part of me wanted to emulate these voices, to merge with them, as if this would finally allow me to remember the streets of my childhood. As much as I tried, though, I had not the power to summon vivid memories of the city. The pinch of remembrance I sometimes felt was unreliable, a doubtful déjà vu too elusive to yield a fulfilling yearning for the past. I could neither recognize these vaguely familiar streets nor hanker after their glorious past. All I did was long for an impossible longing.

It was in this mood of frustrated nostalgia that I stopped at the entrance to the building that once housed Uncle Victor's clinic. A short gallery of shop windows led to the open doors and the lobby. Bathed in neon light, two mannequins stared at me through the glass: one, with a head full of hair, wore a tuxedo; the other, bald as a baby, a plain suit. To their left, above the entrance to the lobby, hung a row of signs, all in Arabic except for that of Dr. A. Aswany, a dentist with an MS from Chicago. The bedraggled entrance made me think there was much wisdom in my uncle's refusal to return, if for nothing else, at least for sparing him the depressing sight of the entrance to his beloved clinic. Number 37, where my father's clinic had been, was no better.

The proximity of the two clinics released in me involuntary memories of my father's acrimonious invectives against his older brother. My father was jealous of his older brother; he envied him his primogeniture. As he repeatedly declares in the diary he wrote while circumnavigating the coast of Africa, my father dreamt of being his father's favorite. "I feel for my father an immense love and admiration," he wrote, "and of all my brothers, I resemble him the most. I was proud to show myself by his side. I see him with silvery hair and his moustache à la Fouad I. I admired the way he carried himself, his elegant gait, and the way he crossed his legs when he sat down. There was something noble and aristocratic about his attitude that commanded immediate respect. In the twenties, when such things were fashionable, he always went to work in a red tarboosh. He carried an ebony walking stick with a silver handle carved in the shape of a lion's head. Self-taught, he spoke Arabic, French, English, and Italian fluently, and he read widely. He was kind and generous, and worked hard to give us the best education available. It cost him a fortune to send me to Paris to study medicine, yet he did it enthusiastically, without a complaint. He was a good man, and a pious one, and I don't mean just on the High Holidays. Every morning and every evening he strapped his tefillin around his arm and prayed, and he was customarily called up to read the Torah on Saturdays and High Holidays. My brother and I would stand while he read, and when he came down we kissed his hands and he blessed us. My father was also a devoted son. His respect and affection for his own father had no limits. It must have been sometime around 1926 that his father died, and the news put my father in a dark mood for a very long time. Papa rarely talked about his father. I have only a vague recollection of my grandfather from when I was a little boy. He lived in a big house in Haret el-Yahoud, the old Jewish quarter. A male nurse took care of him, as he was too old to support himself on his feet. A pointy white beard adorned his chin, and though he seemed to be very old, there was something childish about his behavior. He would throw himself avidly over the bonbons my father brought him. On Sundays my father was in the habit of taking my two older brothers and me in a horse-drawn carriage to the big house in the Jewish quarter. All dressed up, my grandfather would be waiting for us lying on the sofa. Papa kissed the old man's hand first, and then each of us, by order of age, followed suit. Then he would bless us. The old man resembled my brother Victor. My father's predilection for Victor was in my opinion due more to this resemblance than to the fact that he was the firstborn. He doted on Victor so much that we nicknamed him Prince of Wales. My brother may have looked like my grandfather, but, of all my brothers, I was the one who resembled our father the most, and I think he was proud of it. I was like my father in all respects. I feel myself to be the inheritor of his philosophy of life, of the traditions passed on to him by our ancestors. Victor is nothing like him. My father would often tell my mother that when he was young he was just like me. 'I have the impression,' he once told her, 'of looking at myself when I look at Albert.'"

Only after someone bumped against me did I awaken to the fact that I had been obstructing the entrance to 37 Soliman Pasha. The dummies were still staring at me. There was something pitiful about their frozen bodies forever imprisoned in their glass cage. Disturbed by their vacant gaze, I turned away and walked up the avenue toward Adly Street. Along the way it struck me that, not unlike the dummies in the window, my father and uncle had been caged together for life. Sibling rivalry had precluded escape. My father raged against his older brother's alleged mismanagement of their inheritance. Uncle Victor's primogeniture had conferred upon him the trusteeship of their father's sizable estate, not all of which had been distributed before my father left Egypt. A large portion of my grandfather's fortune was in real estate, which my uncle, being the last to leave, was to sell along with the carpets, silverware, and jewelry his brothers and sisters had left behind. Uncle Victor did sell almost everything, and what he couldn't, Aunt Isabelle managed to smuggle out of Egypt. Aunt Isabelle's Swiss passport allowed her to travel to Europe and back, and on each trip she hid silverware and jewelry in the lining of her daughter's stroller. Although my uncle and aunt had gone to great lengths to get my father's share to him, he was less than grateful to them. He claimed that Victor had cheated him out of a good chunk of his inheritance and gambled it in the stock market. Uncle Victor, who may or may not have been guilty, endured his accusations with avuncular good humor. He would lift his eyebrows in a grimace of resignation and say that my father had always been prone to exaggeration. In spite of all this bickering, though, I remember them shuffling through Washington Square Park, arm in arm, bursting into complicitous laughter over some obscure piece of gossip.

Now facing the Adly Street synagogue, I found myself missing the two old men whose overbearing presence I had so often shunned. The upper reaches of the neo-pharaonic synagogue, its huge palmettes and towers bright against the late afternoon sky, loomed over me like an apparition. The temple's gates would soon open to let through the happy procession of people I longed to see. My mother would come out in her white gown flanked by my grandfather in his summer suit and my grandmother in her mink fur. My father and uncle would follow, their hats bobbing this way or that to the tune of their argument. And behind them would come my paternal grandparents, whom I knew so little, followed by Aunt Foufy and her dapper husband.

I hurried across the street to greet them. But when I reached the other side, the heavy wooden doors remained shut. A man in a white uniform with a machine gun appeared from nowhere and asked me for identification. He opened my passport and looked down at my picture, then up at my face, and down again at my picture, until I myself began to doubt my authenticity. Finally satisfied, he returned my passport and told me in English, as best he could, that the synagogue was closed. If I wished to visit I would have to call the offices of the Jewish Community of Cairo. I thanked him and turned back toward Cherif Pasha Street, where Carmen Weinstein, the head of the Jewish Community, had her offices in her family's stationery store. I walked until I saw the faded letters of Carmen's family name painted on a sun-bleached placard over the store's entrance. A mixture of apprehension and shyness stopped me from going inside, but I caught a glimpse of the interior as I passed by. It was narrow and poorly lit with half-empty shelves and a wooden counter, the worn surface of which bore the melancholy beauty of old age and neglect. Passing the store I walked to the end of the block and walked back, but still lacking the courage to step inside, I decided to return to the hotel.

I cannot say with certainty why I had been unable to step into Carmen's store. My best guess is that I feared closure. Once I walked through her door I would go to Bassatine, and once I saw my mother's grave I would have to accept her death. My journey back to the past would end, and, my journey ended, there would no longer be any purpose to pursue. I suppose this fear of emptiness had crept in as soon as I arrived in Cairo and had grown overwhelming when I approached Carmen's shop, so much so that for the next two days I did not venture outside the Marriott grounds. I paced around my room, walked from one end of the terrace to the other, visited the topiary in the garden, strode along the promenade, lost myself in the luxurious neo-Moorish parlors, drank large quantities of coffee in the cafés, examined the souvenirs in the shops, rode the elevator to other floors of the hotel, and haunted the corridors like a pitiful old ghost who no longer scared anyone. Only on the third day was I finally able to pull myself together.

It was on a Monday, if memory serves me well, that I returned to Ismailieh. I first went to the old Fouad Street in search of my grandfather's store, the exact address of which I was unable to secure. My relatives remembered only that Gad & Leon Acher, my grandfather's fabrics shop, stood on the corner of a side street neighboring Cicurel. It was at Cicurel, the most famous of the grand department stores, that my grandfather found employment as a young Turkish immigrant, and it was there that for fifteen long years he had learned his trade. Cicurel was the Galleries Lafayette of Egypt, a store in which everything from fine crockery to the latest Parisian fashions could be bought. My uncle's friends marveled at Cicurel and Fouad Street, in its heyday the Champs-Élysées of Cairo, and they never ceased to bemoan the boulevard's postrevolutionary decay. The *Lonely Planet* agrees. "The biggest store on the street," the guide claims, "is now the kitsch-filled, state-owned Omar Effendi, the Kmart of Egypt."

I spent the morning combing the streets near Cicurel for the large windows that had once displayed the luxurious fabrics my grandfather imported from Europe. The only surviving image of his shop is a photograph within a photograph, a framed picture that hung in his store in São Paulo. I have only a cloudy and dubious remembrance of the sign bearing the store's name above its windows. I have no memory of its exterior. But I do remember sitting on its carpet, feeling the soft pile under my thighs, and tracing its arabesques with my finger. I remember my grandfather lifting me onto the polished top of the wooden counter and asking me where I wished to go for our afternoon walk. I remember giggling in anticipation, imagining the fun I would have walking, my hand in his, along some crowded street to buy a plastic scimitar, or a pistol, or a cowboy's hat, and always, unfailingly, a small bag of my favorite licorice pipes. And I can still summon the smell of his cologne filling the air inside his store or his car—the long-snouted Plymouth in which he took my sister and me to the pyramids on Sunday afternoons. He too sang old French songs, but his favorite was an Italian song of which I can sing only a few lines:

Lo sai che i papaveri son alti, alti, alti,
E tu sei piccolino, e tu sei piccolino
Lo sai che I papaveri son alti, alti,alti,
Sei nato paperino, che cosa ci puoi far

We rode camels in the dunes around Keops, and on our way back we stopped, hot and dusty, at an open-air restaurant illuminated with garlands of light bulbs to drink icy lemonades in the cool evening breeze that blew from the Nile. On these occasions my grandfather laughed a great deal, but though he seemed cheerful and happy, I had the strange impression that he was also on the verge of tears. I remember the confusion this caused me and the compulsion I felt to console him in spite of his apparent happiness. It was as if his joy were irrevocably stained with sorrow. Perhaps my sister and I reminded him of the daughter he had lost. Perhaps the memory made him feel, at one and the same time, the joy of the shared moment and the painful awareness that it would soon pass.

Sometime in the early afternoon I quit looking for my grandfather's shop. To assuage my guilt I held on to the thought that, even if I had known the exact location, nothing of the old store would be left, and I walked away from Fouad Street determined to meet Carmen Weinstein. If nothing else, I would at least make sure to visit my mother's grave. Cherif Pasha Street and Carmen's stationery store were within walking distance.

This time I did not vacillate. With a riotous heart in my chest, I stepped inside the musty store and greeted the young woman behind the counter. She nodded knowingly and without saying a word, went to the back of the store, where she disappeared behind a narrow door. Shortly thereafter Carmen and her mother entered the room through the same door and made their way toward me.

Mother and daughter were a study in contrast. Frail and stooping, the mother was barely visible above the counter; whereas, rotund and erect, the daughter towered over it. They exchanged inquisitive sideways glances as they walked toward me but seemed to relax as I introduced myself and explained that my mother, Odette Cohen, was buried in Bassatine. No sooner had I mentioned my mother's name than Carmen's face lit up in recognition. She remembered the ornate Arabic calligraphy on the marble plaque my uncles and aunts had recently commissioned. That plaque and the equally ornate plaques they placed on my paternal grandparents' tombs had evidently made a memorable impression. Carmen then launched into the contemporary history of Bassatine, recounting how it had been nearly destroyed by squatters and how it had taken her two decades to expel them and build a wall around the cemetery. Carmen spoke matter-of-factly about her travails, emphasizing the kindness of those who had helped her. She didn't brag about the heroic effort it must have taken a Jewish woman in Cairo to oust hundreds of squatters, clean up the dilapidated cemetery, and raise the money to build miles of wall to protect the hallowed grounds.

The next day I returned to the stationery store shortly after lunch. Carmen had told me she would hire a car to drive us to the cemetery. The same smiling clerk greeted me and led the way through the narrow door to Carmen's office. The young woman invited me to sit in a corner armchair, and then disappeared down the shadowy hallway. On the walls of the office, large stains in various shades of brown formed surprisingly beautiful patterns. Books, folders, penholders, calendars, ashtrays, Kleenex boxes, and bottles covered the desks, and a variety of lotion dispensers and perfume vials peered from the open door of one of the cabinets. Framed pictures of Sadat and Mubarak, in washed-out hues of pink and blue, and a multitude of calendars hung on the wall over the desks. This manifold clutter, a veritable cabinet of curiosities, distracted me for a good quarter of an hour until the clerk came back with a cup of coffee and a glass of water. She adroitly lifted glass and cup from the copper tray and placed them on the coffee table. When she left, I moved toward the desk to take a closer look at a picture of a moonlit avenue of sphinxes, but Carmen walked into the office before I could do so. She apologized for being late, and in her no-nonsense way motioned me to follow her outside, where a black limousine waited for us.

Carmen and I sat in the back, and a thin man with a pencil moustache, probably a plainclothesman, sat beside the chauffeur. The men turned and nodded politely. Carmen issued instructions in Arabic, and the driver pulled away into the chaotic traffic. We were soon lost in a maze of streets, where cars mingled with carts and donkeys. I reached for my camera and took a picture of a group of schoolchildren, who rewarded me with waves of the hand and heart-warming grins. I kept on photographing people until the pencil minarets of Muhammad Ali mosque appeared in the distance. Ghostly lines in the hazy sky, they jutted out of the Citadel just as they did in the background of an old picture of my father and sister. In the photograph they face each other, she smiling adoringly at him, he with the usual Gauloise in the corner of his mouth, and in the space between them, the shadow of the

Citadel appears in the distant horizon. The sudden remembrance of my dead sister's smile, a dimpled grin of unfettered joy, filled me with anguish and blinded me momentarily to the world.

I came to only as we approached the spur of the Mokattam Hills on which rise the ramparts of the Citadel. The car turned southward and sped along the road to Maadi. To the left, the barren hills of Mokattam rose to wall Cairo from the desert. The cemetery could not be far. In the photographs of Bassatine, the Mokattam Hills towered over the graves at about the same distance they now appeared to be from the car. Not long after we passed the Citadel the driver veered into a narrow one-lane road flanked on either side by deserted sandy yards. Large sections of the yards' walls had crumbled into mounds of rubble that followed us for miles, a wasteland of dust and stone through which the narrow ribbon of asphalt cleared a path to Bassatine.

Nauseated by the stifling heat, I leaned back against the seat. Just then a car zoomed by my window and swerved into our lane, forcing the driver to step on the brakes. Carmen and I were pitched forward. Our driver slammed the horn and stuck his head out of the window to yell insults at the other driver. When he finally retracted his head back into the car, he continued to mumble imprecations under his breath until, realizing he wasn't alone, he turned around and extended his apologies to Carmen. Carmen nodded, patted her hair, and adjusted herself in her seat. His apologies accepted, the driver sped up across the desolate landscape, and I, somewhat shaken by the incident, couldn't help but think I might have been buried alongside my mother in Bassatine. Some superstitious soul might then have conjectured that, since there are no accidents, this was my fate. It had been written in the big book up in the sky that I would die in near proximity to my mother's grave and thus rejoin her in, or rather, under, the sands of Bassatine.

A few minutes later the car crawled along a dirt path and pulled up to a large green metal gate. A Star of David hung on each of the gate's panels, and on either side of the entrance, stone rubble mixed with refuse lay heaped against the wall. We got out of the car and Carmen pounded on the gate. The gate's hinges screeched, and a bronzed, wrinkled man with yellow teeth peered out from behind the gate. He greeted us and squeezed between the panels in his ankle-long gown, then turned around and pushed against the heavy door. The metal panel rattled along the bumpy ground and stopped dead against a stone. Throwing his weight repeatedly against the metal, the old man tried his best to move the door, but soon gave up and waved us in through the narrow opening between the panels.

On the other side the cemetery fanned out, a flat and sandy patch of land studded with hundreds upon hundreds of ruined slabs of bare limestone. The Mokkatam Hills rose high before us, sloping down to our right to join the brick buildings and giant cranes that flanked the far end of the cemetery.

Not a cloud feathered the sky. We walked toward the line of dwellings cresting the hills, a film of dust over our shoes. Twenty feet away, before a freestanding wall, lay the three graves, my grandparents' to the left, my mother's to the right. Our family name was painted in large letters on the side of her tomb, their vivid green a futile promise of verdant gardens in the afterlife. As we approached the grave, a man appeared from behind us, lifted a bucket full of water, and splashed the large marble plate inscribed in Arabic with my mother's name and dates. I knew of this ritual, though not of its origins or meaning, yet the gesture both startled and angered me, as if the warden had slapped my mother awake. Restraining an impulse to curse him aloud, I studied the elaborate calligraphy that named my mother. When I felt calmer, I looked up and took in the cemetery.

I was at once awed by the austere beauty of the ancient site and dispirited by the inevitability of its doom. The ring of giant cranes besieging the walls would one day burst through. Buildings, streets, roads, and viaducts would bury the holy site, and sweaty pilgrims, camera straps around their necks, would look for the plaque marking what once had been the entrance to Bassatine Cemetery. I stood immobile, facing my mother's grave, unable to digest the horror I felt at the transience of life. My journey seemed futile; I had come all the way to Bassatine to find nothing but stone and dust. Why had I come? How much of my mother could be left under this slab of stone?

With a gentle tap on my shoulder, Carmen asked me if I wished to visit the chapel where the family of the deceased gathered before the burial. I can no longer remember in which direction we walked, or where the chapel stood in relation to the grave, only that it was not too far. Partly roofless, the chapel was a small, boxy structure with two barred windows, each with a Star of David encrusted in its center. Where the roof should have been, only ugly metal rods protruded into the sky.

Through a wide arch I entered the chapel alone. I turned into the dim room where the family had gathered around my mother's body and walked along the walls trying to reconstitute the scene in my mind. I saw them enter the room slowly, one by one, in dark suits: first my grandfather, then my father, and, finally, my uncles. They lined up in front of the wall and gazed at the folds of the cloth that covered her body. The rabbi muttered his prayers and rent their shirts. My grandfather's face stood out among the others, his eyes begging I know not whom for his daughter's life. Overwhelmed by his sorrow, I was gripped by an urge to console him, to put my arms around him. But my eyes blurred, and I could no longer see him. Obeying some obscure instinct, I walked toward the wall where he had been standing, and, my face almost touching it, I caressed its scarred surface with the tips of my fingers. The old wall was warm to the touch. As I felt its bruises and blemishes, I saw my grandfather crying on his knees, and I, too, began to cry.

I had reached the end of my journey. I could not push beyond the wall to an irrecoverable past. And yet, the sense of futility and despair I had felt before my mother's grave softened, and all at once I became aware with a mixture of sorrow and joy, as surprising as it was sweet, that my mother had always been near my sister and me. I realized, as I never had before, that, mediumlike, my grandfather had channeled my mother. She had lived in my grandfather's touch, his voice, his laughter, and in the warmth of his arms. My father and grandmother loved us in their own ways, but my grandfather had loved us like my mother would have. Whether he knew it or not, and though he rarely spoke of her, because of him we know her. Not in the same way people who grow older with their mothers know them, but perhaps in the same way a mystic knows God. It still saddens me now and then to think that I will never remember my mother's smile or the comfort of her embrace. But there are days, now, that are graced with a radiant light, days when my heart bursts with an inexplicable love for the world.

Photographic Credits

Page 4: Spanish-Portuguese Cemetery, Manhattan. © Lindsay Wright.

Page 12: Adly Synagogue, Cairo. © Editions du Scribe.

Page 15: Zeppelin over Cairo. © Lehnert & Landrock, Cairo.

Page 16: Cinema Metro in Flames. © Al-Ahram Weekly.

Page 23: David Hockney, "My Mother, Bolton Abbey, Yorkshire Nov. 1982." Photographic Collage. © David Hockney.

Page 33: Antico Cemitero Israelitico, Venice. © Graziano Arrici.

Page 33: Antico Cemitero Israelitico, Venice. © Graziano Arrici.

Page 42: Mohammed Ali Club. Courtesy of Samir Raafat (egy. com).

Page 44: Cairo, 1910. © Editions du Scribe.

Page 51: Casa Israelitica di Riposo, Venice. © Graziano Arrici.

Page 52: Jacques Louis David, *Bonaparte Crossing the Great Saint Bernard Pass*, 1801. © Eric Lessing/Art Resources, NY.

Page 62: *Esperia* in Venice. Courtesy of Reuben Goosens (www. ssmaritime.com).

Page 63: Titian, *Assumption of the Virgin*. © Alinari/Art Resources, NY.

Page 68: Praça do Patriarca. Photograph by Theodor Preising. Courtesy of Douglas Aptekman (Brasilantigo.com.br).

Page 76: El-Alamein Cemetery. Photograph by Hurley Frank. © National Library of Australia.

Page 77: Sunshield Tank Camouflage. Courtesy of Richard Stokes (maskelynemagic.com).

Page 78: Baudrot. AAHA Collection. Courtesy of Sandro Manzoni (aaha.ch).

Page 78: Jaspers Maskelyne. Courtesy Channel 4 (channel4.com).

Page 87: Scarab Amulet. © Shire Publications.

Page 87: Dung Beetle. Photograph by Dewet (commons. wikimedia.org/wiki/File:Dungbeetle.jpg).

Page 89: Dynastes Hercules. Photograph by Sarefo (commons. wikimedia.org/wiki/File:Dynastes Hercules.jpg).

Page 94: Fabric Merchant. Salonika Postcard. The Ben-Zvi Institute, Jerusalem.

Page 96: Smyrna Citizens trying to catch the Allied ships during the Smyrna Massacre, 1922. Benaki Museum (en.wikipedia .org/ wiki/Greek_genocide).

Page 107: Max Ernst, *Stratified Rock gift of nature composed of gneiss lava Icelandic moss 2 varieties of bladderwort 2 varieties of perineal damcrack cardiac vegetation (b) the same in polished casket more expensive.* Collage with gouache. © 2010 Artists Rights Society (ARS), New York/ADAGP, Paris.

Page 108: Max Ernst and Hans Arp, *Here Everything is Floating.* Pasted photo engravings and pencil. © 2010 Artists Rights Society (ARS), New York/ADAGP, Paris/ VG Bilkunst, Bonn.

Page 113: Soliman Pasha Square. Orient Pictures Archive.

Page 115: Shepheard's Hotel. Thomas Cook Archives.

Page 124: Fouad I Street. © Lehnert & Landrock, Cairo.